GOING IT ALONE

You are Tim Murphy, and no one can help you.

Not Paula, your wife, who thinks she knows and loves you, but can never know what Vietnam meant to you and did to you.

Not Luke, your buddy, who can swap his tales of 'Nam with you, but can't let you into his secret heart anymore than you can let him into yours.

Neither of them—not the wife who loves the good and gentle man she thinks you are, nor the friend who has his own war to wage—can go back with you to face that piece of your past that has refused to die—and is now trying to kill you. . . .

See the Movie, Read the Book in SIGNET and MENTOR Editions

CEASE FIRE

A NOVEL BY
Jack Casey

BASED UPON THE SCREENPLAY BY
George Fernandez

A SIGNET BOOK

NEW AMERICAN LIBRARY

NAL BOOKS ARE AVAILABLE AT QUANTITY DISCOUNTS WHEN USED
TO PROMOTE PRODUCTS OR SERVICES. FOR INFORMATION PLEASE
WRITE TO PREMIUM MARKETING DIVISION, NEW AMERICAN LIBRARY,
1633 BROADWAY, NEW YORK, NEW YORK 10019.

PUBLISHER'S NOTE

This novel is a work of fiction. Names, characters, places, and
incidents either are the product of the author's imagination or,
if real, used fictitiously.

SIGNET TRADEMARK REG. U.S. PAT. OFF. AND FOREIGN COUNTRIES
REGISTERED TRADEMARK—MARCA REGISTRADA
HECHO EN CHICAGO, U.S.A.

SIGNET, SIGNET CLASSIC, MENTOR, PLUME, MERIDIAN and NAL BOOKS
are published by New American Library,
1633 Broadway, New York, New York 10019

First Printing, August, 1985

2 3 4 5 6 7 8 9

PRINTED IN THE UNITED STATES OF AMERICA

The Viet Nam War took the lives of over 58,000 Americans between 1960 and 1975. Over 2,500 Americans are still missing.

Since their return over 50,000 veterans have died in peacetime.

Cease Fire is dedicated to the spirit of life and to those who returned, their wives and their children.

Foreword

I did not go to Viet Nam. Whoever pulled numbers out of the drum pulled 333 for my birthday, so at nineteen I was allowed to study literature. I still marvel at the amount of literature devoted to war. That year—1970—they closed down the university—Yale University—because of Viet Nam, because the National Guard shot four students in Ohio.

I didn't go to Viet Nam, but I brooded on it and I had a lot of friends who did go. Many of them came back, some of them came back whole. Back then I watched our American culture polarized over a war. I had no stomach for carrying signs, there were too many causes. I studied war in literature, then I left the country. In 1974 I returned, and I believed there might be hope, and there was hope because I had met June.

Timothy Murphy, the hero of this book, was in Viet Nam in 1970, the year they closed Yale, but the story deals with him today, grown up, a family man. George Fernandez wrote and filmed this story and asked me if I would turn it into a novel. George did go to Viet Nam, and his story is a powerful one, a true one because it tells about the long and difficult odyssey "home."

Mr. Fernandez was fortunate in his choice of a male lead in *Cease Fire*. Don Johnson summons precisely the brooding, turbulent passions that evoke the sensitivity and the struggles of Timothy Murphy.

In its way, this is an epic story, a story of forces of light—reason, forgiveness, trust and love—battling forces of darkness and guilt, despair, and self-hatred. The forces of light and life must at last overcome the forces of darkness and death. That is what the literature of war tells us, and what the memorial in Washington stands for. By bringing to this work what I've seen and read and learned and felt, I've tried to augment George Fernandez's powerful story, and to explore those troubled, sensitive emotions portrayed by Don Johnson on the screen.

The Timothy Murphy of this story is someone we all know, the ordinary guy next door who tries to do the right thing, who swears and drinks beer, who loves his wife and his kids, yet who must at last confront an unspeakable horror. The theme of his story engenders hope for us all, for anytime a man confronts impossible odds, he should be admired. But when he wins, well, that is why we hold our babies to the sun.

Jack Casey

Troy, New York
June 29, 1985

Chapter 1

If he tried, he could remember an earlier time, but it seemed dreamlike, misty, unreal. He didn't often think back to life before, but when he did, there were hot cars, surfboards, rock'n'roll music, gulls screaming, and warm, tender girls, blond girls with tanned skin running freely along beaches where waves burst from the sea. There were palm trees swaying in a dark, full wind, crackling campfires, cold beer and sing-alongs. And infusing his life with hope, there was an overriding promise, as vague as it was certain, that an important destiny awaited him.

Timothy Murphy had been something of an all-American boy, the type of bright, handsome, athletic young man that every mother hoped her daughter would have the sense to marry. His eyes sparkled with wit and promise. His sense of humor always found the fun and joy in a tough situation. His quick,

9

supple mind grasped the essence of problems and issues, thought rapidly to conclusions. He was not lazy. His only mistake was that he was a romantic; he thought the good times in the sun would last forever.

Timothy Murphy brought few of his promising qualities with him to manhood. He had been drafted for Viet Nam, and he served a thirteen-month stint "in-country." When he returned, he was only twenty-one, but his bright eyes had lost their luster. He tried not to draw people's attention to himself. He tried to live quietly and apart. He tried to be happy. He married and had children. But if caught in a thoughtful moment, a smoldering intensity gleamed in his eye, his teeth clenched, and his brow furrowed, as if the ancient mysteries he had witnessed in-country must be endlessly explored, but never, ever shared.

A photograph of four young men, smiling against a background of banyan trees and elephant grass, once told of a lark four buddies shared long ago. There was little to smile about then, but they all believed that joy could be found among the suffering and the sorrow if you didn't dwell on your misery, if you looked elsewhere for happiness and hope, if you thought of home. The photograph would be convincing, too, if you did not know what happened in 'Nam. They had four copies of that picture made, blown up and printed so each of them would remember. Timothy Murphy, stood third from the left, wearing his headband, the Black Halo. His copy of the picture, though, was missing one of the four men. Long ago he had deliberately ripped away the image of the fellow on the right, the image of Badman, the fellow on the far right. Then Timothy Murphy stored the photograph away with his war medals so he would never forget, and also so he would never have to look at it again.

In Viet Nam, Timothy Murphy learned that fear is the most powerful drug. He learned it quickly, he learned it well, and he learned it forever. Cold, raw fear numbed him like a narcotic. It engendered hallucinations and fantasies of unspeakable horror. It widened and narrowed his eye, flared his nostril, sensitized his ear to hear, beyond the stout beating of his own heart, the sound of another breathing. Like a machete blade through vines and brush, fear cut through love, hate, trust, anger, greed, hunger, thirst, sexual craving, through the joy and camaraderie, through the agony and sorrow he had shared with other men in arms. Simple fear, ordinary, everyday fear. With the intensity of a surgical laser it pierced through the muscle and membranes and tissues of all he had ever believed life to be, and it fixed for him a new vision of life—a shivering, wriggling, reptilian vision of life that brought rage when its clammy hand touched his thoughts and loathing when it breathed its foul breath upon his feelings.

And the jungle was fear itself. By day the lush greenery beneath the jungle canopy, the faraway crying of birds and gibbons and spider monkeys, the steamy toil of trees and vines to reach skyward, to suck at air and sun, the quiet, deceptive jungle crawled with a thousand possibilities of death—punji stakes, antipersonnel mines, booby traps, the imminent danger of a sniper's bullet or a full-blown firefight. But night was worse, far worse. At night the jungle seethed with dark energy. It was not Charlie's ingenuity, not his ferocity or his treachery in ambush that made grown men cry themselves to sleep, that brought on dread and the sickening fear that the red tropical sun would never again shoot up above the eastern treetops. It was Charlie's mere presence that caused the nervous twitch about the lip, the squinting of the eye, the sleepless chatter and the sweat. Timothy Murphy was never dry during his entire tour of duty. Sweat poured from him by day and chilled him by night, sweat and fear together every waking, sleepless hour.

And Charlie, the Viet Cong, the enemy—a boyish figure with flat brown Oriental eyes and cropped hair, dressed in black pajamas, appearing and vanishing out of the jungle like an angel of death to pluck whomever he would take, or to maim and cripple whomever he wanted to punish with suffering far worse than death, or perhaps to snatch away prisoners to a place where torture administered with grim Oriental patience transformed strong men into whimpering pups. Charlie. A friendly, casual name, like your bowling or golfing buddy, the godfather of your kids, your uncle, a name, part understatement, part irony, bestowed by Americans upon a resourceful, crafty, relentless horde of guerrilla warriors. Charlie always lurked beyond the next turn of the path, behind the paddy dike where water buffalo wallowed. Charlie lay under the flooring mats of hootches. He watched from the trees. He tunneled beneath the jungle floor to vanish out of sight and appear hundreds of meters away in an instant. Charlie was your destiny, the grinning cruel face of your worst nightmare, a personification of the dark, tangled, suffocating jungle of your worst fears.

It seemed they were always in the bush on patrol. Again the helicopter dropped them in a field of elephant grass. Elephant grass was funny because you never knew whether it was three or ten feet deep, and you never knew what punji stakes or booby traps would be waiting for you. As the rotors beat the air, the four of them waded through the swale into the bush. The Huey rose up then, powerful, magnificent, like a camouflaged armored truck rising bodily into heaven.

Rafer, a young black kid from east Los Angeles, checked the compass reading and pointed into the jungle with the barrel of his M-16. Corporal Timothy Murphy scanned the treeline and frowned. You knew they were there, but you could never see them. "Let's go!" he whispered hoarsely, not looking at the others. Crouching low, weapons at the ready before them, the four moved into the silent jungle. Occasional sunbeams pierced the high canopy and filtered in rays through the steamy air. The solemnity was that of a cathedral, but these men were not pondering another world. Eyes, ears, nostrils strained for some trace of Charlie, some telltale sign of where, when, or how the slumbering green profusion of life would erupt in flame and explosion and blood. Yet the quiet wind yielded no clue.

Warily the four approached a clearing of conical straw hootches surrounding a yard, an unextinguished fire smoldering into the air. Was Charlie hiding, or had he fled? Gingerly the four prodded doors open with the barrels of their weapons, squinting to pierce the gloom within, expecting every instant an explosion, volleys of automatic-weapons fire. Sanchez pointed to the well covered by a sheet of corrugated metal.

"Stay away from there," Badman cautioned them. A buzzing sound came from the well. "Stay away, man!" But Sanchez and Rafer cautiously walked to the well and slid off the top. They stood at the lip of the well, looking down, all caution forgotten.

"Oh, mannn!" Rafer groaned.

"Don't go over there," Timothy Murphy told himself, yet his feet did not obey. A curiosity, a fascination drew him. What was in that pit? A store of rice? Weapons? Refugees? "Don't look! Don't look!" Timothy Murphy's mind screamed, yet the fascination drew him to the very edge of the edge of the pit, and slowly he peered in.

Timothy Murphy bolted upright in bed, his eyes bulging, his mouth gulping and gasping for air, sweat streaming down his face, soaking the sheets beneath his thighs and buttocks and calves. Slowly, methodically, he catalogued the room: a dresser, a chair, the closet door ajar, the kids' portraits on the nightstand, the glowing dial of the clock radio. Home, he thought, *home.* The ordinary furniture and objects of this small bedroom comforted him. Although it recurred, the nightmare ended. There was a time, he remembered, gazing at Paula's sleeping form, when the nightmare wouldn't end; it only got worse. Fondly Tim brushed a strand of Paula's blond hair away from her forehead. He felt sick at heart seeing the reflection of the orange clock dial in her eye. Paula was awake! Paula had seen! Paula knew!

He stared at her. She stared at him. Neither spoke. Paula's lips trembled, her eyes imploringly searched his. Timothy Murphy suddenly felt very thirsty. He peeled back the sheet, stepped out of bed, and walked to the bathroom for a glass of water.

The Murphys lived in Miami and although Tim had not always lived there, and probably would not always live there, he lived in Miami as he lived his life, for the moment, forgetting about yesterday, hardly thinking about tomorrow. At the edge of the long sandy Florida peninsula, Miami suited Tim Murphy. Facing the broad, sunny Atlantic, its skyline thrusting proudly above the beach, Miami boldly met each sunrise, each new day. Yet behind the city, to the north and west, stretched the vast, desolate waste of the Everglades.

As a child, Tim had fished with his uncle in the Everglades. The brooding trees hung with Spanish moss, the winding, meandering streams that twisted back upon themselves, the lush growth that turned rank and rotten, and above all, the strange creatures that lurked in the trees, in the bush, beneath the surface of the water, old creatures, wrinkled, reptilian creatures, lizards, alligators, ancient turtles, and mammoth snakes, the creatures had given the Everglades a sense of mystery, of enchantment back then. Sitting in a frail shell of a boat with his uncle, dangling a fishing line below the green scum of the water, it was always an excitement to conjure in his mind what would bite, what he'd haul into the boat. Now the Everglades repelled him. Although he longed sometimes to reenter that lush and strange and wondrous realm of boyhood memories, he had seen too much jungle elsewhere.

His uncle had taken him fishing upon the ocean as well. Once Tim landed a three-hundred-pound marlin, and for a time was a celebrity at his uncle's yacht club. Now he hardly ever went to the beach. Fishing had no appeal for him. Although he loved the graceful arc as the marlin leaped from the waves, majestic and free, he loved when whales breached and sharks harvested schools of anchovies, he saw no point in hauling fish into a boat. Let them swim, let them live. And although he enjoyed swimming, the tanned young girls, the bold, flexing young men with Frisbees and coolers of beer and loud radios, with dune buggies and surfboards revealed to him a sadness too aching and keen.

Currently Tim was unemployed. Although he had "graduated" from the University of Southeast Asia, and his discharge papers were his diploma, Uncle Sam his college dean, Tim lacked an ordinary college degree. Skilled only in the arts and crafts of killing, he held and then abandoned a string of jobs, laboring jobs mostly. He dressed in jeans and sweat shirts and running shoes and he drove an old dented Chevy. He secretly scorned the bright tanned young men in poplin and seersucker suits who drove fast cars, dated fresh pretty young women, and enjoyed Miami's flashy nightlife. When he thought about it at all, he harbored a slight resentment that they had been spared what he had endured.

But Timothy Murphy was not self-pitying by nature. He wanted a simple life. He did not like dining out. He thought dancing was foolish. He did not hanker for the toys, the boats, the cars, stereos and cameras they wanted. He did not want strings of affairs with dashing, exotic women. He wanted to live an ordinary life, to fit in and remain unnoticed. That was why he had married soon after his return and had moved to the other side of town where no one knew him. That was why he insisted on having children immediately. That was why he bought a plain house when he could afford it in a nondescript suburban development. And that was why he hated being unemployed. The unemployed did not fit in.

The unemployment office, like some temple to halfhearted socialism, depressed him utterly. It received supplicants, the poor, huddled masses, then doled out their reward for admitting their humility and need, their inability to break the cycle of dependence by finding work. The shabby offices reeking of cigarette smoke and stale human sweat, the dull, shadowless glow of fluorescent lighting, the scuffed linoleum and chipped Formica counters, but mostly the tangible *despond* of the place caused Tim's pride to bristle. The bored and petulant bureaucrats, ushers and functionaries in the temple, dished out humiliation, methodically extracting the last measure of self-respect before handing over the check.

Self-consciously Timothy Murphy stepped to the end of one of several long lines and bowed his head. It would be half an hour at least. All eyes, he felt, were upon him. The others, those who had been unemployed for months, seemed resigned, like a battalion of the half dead. They didn't notice him, he told himself. They were shrouded by their own miseries. He looked about to confirm his feeling. One old lady in the next line had actually brought a chair and sat reading a book, advancing her chair each time the line moved. Tim sought to find humor in her acceptance of the endless droning: "How long have you been unemployed? ... Have you been actively looking for employment this past month? ... Have you been offered employment? ..." But it only underscored the hopelessness, the endless waiting for a begrudged gift.

Turning back, Timothy's eyes caught a red military insignia, a number one, upon the sleeve of a fatigue jacket. That insignia seemed like a wound. Tim looked at the wearer of the jacket—a slender man in his late thirties who was checking classified ads with his pen. Tim studied him. Was he wearing it in mockery? The man had weathered skin and his black beard was grizzled with white. No, Tim decided, he had been in-country.

Sensing Tim's eyes on him, the man looked up and

caught Tim doing precisely what he'd feared others were doing to him. Tim stared back in embarrassment, his eyes widening. The man smiled and waved hello. Tim quickly turned his head forward toward the counter without returning the greeting. For fifteen minutes he did not look at that military insignia, yet he wanted to—it was fitting that another veteran was here. There had been no lack of work over there, in 'Nam.

"Next!" the woman called at last as Tim stepped forward and lay his form on the counter. The lady, a bored, middle-aged Latin woman, turned the form over, then looked back up at him. "You have to finish filling out the back." She indicated the blank sections, then pointed across the room. "There's a counter over there."

"Uh . . . do you have a pen I could use?" Tim stammered in embarrassment. He had filled out the form at home.

"There are pens on the counter," she said. Again she pointed, thrusting his form back at him. With her other hand she motioned the next in line to step forward.

"Ma'am, señorita, will I have to wait in that line again?" Tim pointed with his thumb. The line had grown even longer since he had started.

With anger and annoyance she looked up. "Look. Just finish filling out the form. Then you can bring it right back to me. Okay?"

Tim nodded, accepted his form back, and walked to the rear of the room. He turned over the form, picked up a pen, and began to write. It was out of ink. Frustrated, he tried another. It was also out of ink. He tried a third, violently scribbling upon a scrap of paper until it ripped. It, too, was out of ink.

The man with the military insignia held up his pen. "Hey, man!" Tim heard, and he looked up. The man tossed it to him.

"Thanks," Tim said, and he smiled, self-conscious, yet relieved.

When he returned to the front of the line, a plump, middle-aged man had replaced the Latin woman at the clerk's window. His complexion was mottled and he had a bureaucratic tightness about the mouth. Timothy Murphy leaned in front of a black woman.

"Oh, we have schedules," the man was saying impatiently to the woman.

"I'm only asking for your help," the woman pleaded. She glared at Tim.

"Excuse me," Tim said. "Excuse me a second. The lady that was here before, well, she said I could bring this right back, so—"

"You're going to have to wait in line like everyone else," the man said impatiently. A superiority gained from knowing and enforcing rules flashed in his eye. He turned back to the black woman.

"But, no," Tim persisted. "You see, I've already waited in line."

"So? What makes you so special?"

Tim ignored the direct challenge, and he spied the Latin woman toward the back of the office. She was sipping coffee and talking on the phone.

"There she is!" he cried. "Excuse me, señorita, could you . . ."

The woman peered up at him, then indifferently looked back to her coffee.

"Look," the man said, "I'm not going to do anything until you go back to the end of the line."

"But," Tim protested, exasperated, "I've already waited in line once!"

Angry at the interruption, the black woman interjected, "I've got a hair appointment." The clerk motioned for the security guard.

"Well, I've got a job interview in fifteen minutes," Tim said. "I can't wait in line again! She told me . . ." But he stopped in midsentence, seeing the clerk's intractable and sneering expression. It was always this way. Tim's eyes narrowed and he fought to control his rage.

"Excuse me, sir"—he heard a gentle, officious voice— "I'm sorry, but you'll have to step to the back of the line." The white-haired guard reached to touch his elbow, but Tim reacted instantly, jerking his arm away, glaring at them with hate and rage. The clerk gulped, and the guard took a step backward. Everyone fell silent, expecting an explosion. Timothy Murphy fought to control himself as his eyes widened and narrowed. Then he threw his form at the clerk and said in a hoarse whisper, "You just take this and shove it up your ass!"

Timothy Murphy spun about and stalked from the counter as an aisle widened for him between two lines of supplicants.

"Hey," called the man in the fatigue coat, "he stole my pen!" His comic expression defused some of the mounting tension, but no one laughed. They shuffled on to the window for their checks as though nothing at all had happened.

Chapter 2

Tim Murphy's sole delight in life was his home. It wasn't a luxurious home. In fact, it was deliberately ordinary in a middle-class development. At home with Paula, his son Ronnie, and daughter Ellen, Tim felt fulfilled, wanted, whole and worthy. Though he talked often about visits to his uncle, he never discussed his own turbulent boyhood, and at times it seemed he'd never had a mother or a father. This turbulence and difficulty he was determined to correct in the next generation of Murphys by instilling in his children a respect and a love of life.

Each child had a pet—Ellen a hamster and Ronnie a puppy—and Timothy made sure they cared for their needs, feeding and cleaning after them. Each child had a small plot of land on the lot to grow flowers or vegetables, and these were scrupulously tilled. Timothy did this to instill in the children a respect for

animal and vegetable life. For their spiritual awareness, Tim insisted they attend church each Sunday,
though he himself went only at Christmas and Easter.
He strongly believed in the moral values imparted by
the Catholicism of his boyhood, yet he had heard
an archbishop's speech in 'Nam advocating an escala-
tion of the war, and he could not square what had
happened there with his belief. He hoped his children
never encountered such a test.

Tim still possessed a strong respect for authority.
This harkened from before his military days, which
had done more to erode, or at least deaden, his respect
for authority than to confirm it. Tim sought to instill
this respect in his children, too, and required their
strict obedience both at home and at school. Yet he
believed authority should not be distant, aloof, scowling, and critical. He believed it should be active and
nurturing, and at times fun. And so he insisted upon
tucking the children in each night.

From the living room this night, Timothy watched
Paula coaxing Ronnie to swallow his cough medicine.
After the argument at the unemployment office, this
simple domestic scene pleased him greatly. His son
was sitting on the kitchen counter, his mouth clamped
shut, and Paula was urging him to open his mouth.
Tim felt as if he were viewing a Norman Rockwell
painting.

"Ronnie," Paula said with determination, "open your
mouth," yet her seriousness was strained. She could
hardly keep from laughing at the sad little upturned
face. Ronnie shook his head no.

"Open your mouth!" Paula repeated more intently.
She urged the spoon between his lips, but Ronnie shook
his head defiantly and hunched down to get away.
"Ronnie, please take the medicine. It's good for you.

It'll make you feel better. You can sleep all night tonight."

This didn't matter to the boy. He looked up and just stared. Now Paula began to assert her authority with impatience.

"I'm telling you, Ronnie, open your mouth. Open it!"

Ellen leaned in to assist. "It's good for you, Ronnie. It tastes like *candy!*"

"Yes, Ronnie," Paula urged. "Like candy!" Ellen's ploy worked and Paula slid the medicine into his mouth.

"Yuk!" Ronnie cried, squinting and pursing his lips sourly. Ellen jumped down from the counter squealing, "I tricked you!" Ronnie chased her.

"I think it's bedtime," Paula called, and Tim took his cue.

"Ahhh!" he cried with upraised eyebrows. "Bedtime!" And he swooped down and picked up a child under each arm.

"Aw, Dad, do we have to?" Ronnie kicked in frustration.

"Yes, you have to." He held the children up to kiss their mother good night, first Ronnie, then Ellen. "Good night, Mom," he urged them to say. "Good night, Mom." Then he leaned and kissed Paula. "Good night, Mom."

Carrying the children under either arm, he turned toward the hallway. "He's at the ten," he called, pretending he was carrying a football. "Will they catch him?" The kids laughed and squealed. "It's the five, the three, will he fumble?" He shook Ronnie, then bounded triumphantly into the children's bedroom and deposited each in a bed. "Touchdown!"

"Good night, Daddy," Ellen said.

"Good night, sweetheart," Tim answered. He went to the door, turned, and happily regarded his children snug in their beds. "We're going to sleep now, right? No parties, no games. On three, you're asleep. One! Two! Three! Sleep!" He flicked off the light, then immediately turned it back on. "You're not asleep!" he called playfully. He turned off the light and began to close the door.

"Hey," Ronnie called, and pointed to his nightlight.

"Oh, yeah. I forgot." Tim crossed the room, pushed on the small light, then leaned over his son and said, "You know, there's nothing to be afraid of." He looked down lovingly.

"I know," Ronnie whispered, but his expression belied his words.

Tim saw he was still chewing gum, and held out his hand. "Gum!"

Ronnie spat the gum into Timothy's cupped hand.

"Yiccchhh!" Tim said with an exaggerated revulsion. Ronnie laughed.

"Good night."

"Good night."

Tim turned for another look at the children. "Pleasant dreams," he said. Gently he closed the door.

His own bedtime was Tim Murphy's favorite time of day. After hours of searching for jobs, trying to sell himself in interviews, trying to outwit secretaries, after a day passed on streets and freeways, in offices of machine plants, warehouses, department stores, after the indifferent bustle of the world had tired him and had reinforced his suspicion that he fit nowhere into the scheme of things, and never would, he sought refuge with Paula. It was there after a good meal and after tucking in the children that he felt intimate, manly, capable, and whole.

Three years younger than Tim, Paula was entering the full bloom of her womanhood. Slender, pert, and very pretty, she had been a confirmed tomboy until puberty interrupted her romping. Her marriage to Tim had rekindled her boyishness and the frolics of their honeymoon matured their furtive premarital sensuality into energetic, healthy, wholehearted, and very intimate play. Childbearing had not noticeably changed Paula's figure. She took pride in her appearance and she exercised daily.

From the first their lovemaking had been strenuous, almost acrobatic. But a change, at first imperceptible, overtook her as she entered sexual maturity. Her appetite and pleasure heightened, and with the increase in her desire, she drew Timothy into uncharted realms of pleasure, and their commitment, their intimacy deepened wonderfully.

This night, Timothy reached bed and slid in above Paula. They had begun to kiss passionately when Tim abruptly stopped and raised his head.

"I forgot," he said.

"What?"

"I have a headache."

Paula laughed playfully. "Get out of here!"

Tim rolled onto his back and stared at the ceiling.

"Okay. Fine," she said. She rolled over to her own side of the bed and snuggled into her pillow as Tim lay next to her with a smirk of anticipation. Paula's hand hit something hard underneath her pillow, and she reached under and pulled out a shoe.

"What's that?" Tim asked in mock surprise. "My goodness, there's a tennis shoe under your pillow!"

"Yeah," she said, puzzled. "With two airplane tickets taped to it."

"Airplane tickets?" Tim shrugged his shoulder, trying to act innocent, and he rolled away from her. Slowly a smile spread across her face.

"Nassau? We can't afford this!" She looked at him "Can we afford it?"

"No," Tim said with determination, "but we're going anyway."

Paula paused to think, then excitedly pounced on him, kissing him again and again.

"Well, well, well." Tim laughed. "My headache just went away."

"Oh, good!" Paula said. Their kisses grew more and more passionate, then suddenly Paula squealed with delight. "I'm so excited!"

Together they laughed and their laughter was mingled, then muffled as their lips met, and they groaned with pleasure. Tim reached up and flicked off the light.

When Tim was laid off, Paula found a job. Money they had set aside soon dried up. Paula dreaded going to work as a waitress. She despised the crude truck drivers and leering salesmen she had to serve. Benny, owner of The Chef's Inn, required his "girls" to wear low-cut uniforms so his customers might flirt and ogle and so not notice the bland and greasy taste of his food. And yet, with the good news about their planned trip to Nassau, a new bounce was in Paula's step.

"Carmen!" she said excitedly. "I just couldn't believe it! Tim said we deserved it, it would help our luck change, and that his uncle Bob would be patient while we pay back the money."

"Blue plate's up!" sounded from the kitchen.

"That's wonderful," Carmen said. "You two have seen a rough year. And you'll have such fun! All you need is a bikini and plenty of tanning oil. You need some color in those cheeks." Playfully Carmen pinched her.

"Blue plate's up! Yo! Carmen!"

Carmen rolled her eyes, sighed, and turned toward the kitchen.

"What the hell's wrong with you—deaf or something?"

"Sorry, Benny." She didn't sound sorry.

"Don't give me the 'Sorry, Benny.' Pick up your orders and get them to my customers before they leave!"

" 'Scuse me." Carrying a plate and utensils, Carmen brushed past Paula. She rolled her eyes. "Boy, he's in a good mood!"

Benny leaned out from the kitchen. "Just move it! Move it!"

"Ah, he's a pussycat." Paula laughed, her cheer undiminished. She turned to her customers at the counter, and a burly truck driver intentionally pushed his spoon off the edge of the counter; it clattered onto the floor. Paula glared at him. "Cute. The old spoon trick!"

"Aw," the man said gruffly, "it ain't so far for you to reach!"

Defiantly Paula thrust her fists upon her hips. Then, as she bent down to pick up the spoon, she glared up at the man and his buddy, who stood up to get a glimpse of her cleavage. As she bent, her blouse parted, further revealing the smooth contours of her breasts. The anger in her eyes only excited the men more, and they laughed lewdly. Paula threw down the spoon in disgust and splattered the two with soup.

The burly driver followed her on his side of the counter to the register. "I left you a tip," he said suggestively.

Paula considered sarcasm, then thought better of it. "Well, thank you."

"I didn't have to, you know, sweetie. Just my way of telling you something."

As she took the check, she deliberately showed him her wedding band. "Like you're sorry?"

The man shrugged. "Well, kind of . . ." He turned to his buddy and shrugged again. "Yeah, I am. Okay. Sorry."

Paula smiled sarcastically, despising the part she needed to play. "Okay," she said in her best motherly voice, "you're forgiven."

The man seemed pleased. "Bye," he said.

"Bye," Paula returned, and angrily, her joy at the Nassau trip obscured by these daily indignities, rang up the sale in the register. If only, if only Tim could find work!

Chapter 3

The Statue of Liberty Bar had a faded, peeling likeness of Lady Liberty hanging above the street out
front. Tubes of neon outlining the lady's form made
her stand out from the night street as a beacon of
hope and comfort for the lonely and homeless. The bar
sat in the middle of a block of storefronts built during
the late forties when a land rush had brought Yankees southward, looking, like Ponce de Leon four cen-
turies before, for the fountain of youth. Neon lights
advertising beer lit the windows night and day. Inside, it smelled of cigarette smoke and stale, spilled
beer, and four old men sat along the bar silently
drinking shots and chasers, remembering better times.

Timothy Murphy had been here an hour. Coming
from another unsuccessful job interview at a used-tire
warehouse, he had paused for a few beers. The place
suited his mood and the fat barmaid, heavily made up

and staggering from her morning "healers," provided
some comic relief. He studied the want ads diligently
and so didn't notice when a slim man in his late
thirties entered and tossed a green fatigue jacket with
a red insignia upon the bar.

"Things are definitely looking up around here," the
man said, though nothing had changed since his visit
the day before. "Patty, you're all teased up."

"Just for you, Luke, honey, just for you." She smiled
and her makeup cracked.

Luke motioned with his fingers about the size of the
bottle he wanted. "Let me have a nice cool one," and
he licked his lips.

Patty blew out cigarette smoke. "Sure, honey, sure."
And she turned and waddled suggestively toward the
beer cooler. Luke looked across the bar and recognized
Timothy Murphy from the unemployment line three
days before. Tim did not look up. One of the old men
belched and Patty scolded him as she brought Luke's
beer to him. Luke tossed a few dollars on the bar and
turned toward Tim.

"Hey, how are you doing?"

Tim stared up, hearing someone speaking to him,
then looked back to his newspaper, not recognizing
Luke.

"That was some bullshit the other day, wasn't it?"

Tim squinted in Luke's direction but still didn't
recognize him. Indifferently he returned to his paper.
"I'm sorry, I don't know what you mean," he muttered.

"I was *there*," Luke persisted. "I was there the other
day at the unemployment office. The other day."

"Oh, yeah," Timothy Murphy said, recognizing him
at last. "You were in the other line."

Luke smiled. "Yeah, I was. I saw that you noticed
my jacket."

"I did," Tim said, remembering. "I did, didn't I?" He considered. He picked up his pen. "I think I owe you a pen." He handed it toward Luke.

"No problem. You can keep it."

Timothy Murphy nodded. They had run out of conversation, and so he went back to his want ads.

"Hey," Luke suggested awkwardly, "can I, can I buy you a beer?"

Timothy eyed him suspiciously.

"Oh." Luke laughed and pointed to a small gold earring in his left ear. "Don't let the earring fool you . . . *thay*-lor," he said with a lisp and limp wrist.

Tim laughed and nodded. "Yeah, sure. I'll have another one."

"Patty," Luke called to the barmaid, "another one over here." He walked around the bar, looked at Tim for a long moment, then asked confidentially, "So, how long were you in 'Nam?"

Timothy regarded him with a suspicious scowl, then looked away. The sudden question had taken him by surprise and he thought a moment before answering slowly, deliberately: "All . . . fucking . . . day."

Luke smiled and nodded at the irony. "Patty, my love, give him another."

Tim looked up, stared at Luke for a long moment. Luke met his gaze evenly. Tim smiled and Luke returned the smile. Tim didn't want to talk about 'Nam. It was a rule he had made and he'd obeyed. Things had been difficult in bars. In fact, they had been so difficult that for five years he had by and large stopped going, because the people he encountered always wanted to know about the war. And when he did go out, he kept to himself and did not talk to anyone. Either scowls of disgust or prying looks had met him when he first returned. The average American considered vets baby killers and civilian rapers. Some wanted to know all about the gore and the violence and the fear and the drugs, and they asked stupid questions and weren't satisfied with one-word answers.

When he had first returned, Timothy Murphy sometimes went to the Colorado Bar, a corner bar much like this one, with two other vets. They talked about being in-country. They sat and sipped their golden beer in the long afternoon and enjoyed the silent camaraderie of knowing they were together and no one would ask the others to share their private visions of hell exported from 'Nam. One friend, Will, had his testicles blown off when his jeep ran over a mine. He had a slight limp now. Before his tour of duty he had been quite a hit with the ladies, but now he let his hair grow long and shaggy, as if he wanted to hide from the world, and he lived on his disability and stayed drunk and stoned. The other, Fred, had received a dum-dum bullet through his arm, rendering it eighty-percent disabled. Fred enjoyed the way the VA hospital doctors measured the percentage of use you could lose from your arm, and how they would pay compensation accordingly.

In drinking with them, Timothy Murphy came to appreciate their laughs. These two had a particular laugh that at first annoyed him, then pleased him, and finally scared him so that he avoided them. It wasn't a belly laugh, it was a snicker or a giggle. They both had it down pat. Neither had a job, neither had a girlfriend. They did not go to parties. They drove old, dented cars and lived in the low-rent tenements that Fred dubbed "Desolation Row."

Tim first was annoyed by the laugh because it seemed to be their response to everything. Any statement, any question, any observation would elicit the snicker.

He stopped being annoyed by it when he didn't notice it anymore. For months he drank with them behind the smoky glass, looking out upon the world through a neon sign. He became pleased with the laughter when he began to see through their eyes the absurdity of the world, the useless ambitions and needless complications of family, job, of emotional entanglements and personal commitments. The laugh sufficed as an answer for any request to do something for someone else, for any notion that any action would have any benefit or make any difference in the scheme of things. The laugh symbolized the utter absurdity of returning home, of trying to convey the horror and misery of 'Nam, of trying, in the face of such death and mutilation, to believe in any way that life had meaning, that human life was sacred. Tim became frightened of the laugh one Memorial Day.

Curious to see how the Viet Nam vets would be treated in the Memorial Day parade, Timothy Murphy loafed on a corner of town. The parade began at noon and on came the pageant—VFWs in peaked hats, the Gold Star mothers walking with chests held out patriotically, heroically, the prom queens upon floats, little vestals beckoning with white gloves, the bands and the baton twirlers and the police and firemen and the color guards, and the blaring music echoing off the buildings, winding through the more dilapidated sections of town, the whole thing vaingloriously marching itself to doomsday, but no one particularly noticing, except Timothy Murphy, and no one calling a halt.

He had ducked into the Colorado Bar for a few quiet beers, and Will and Fred were there watching television.

"They had a battalion of soldiers from the army,"

Tim said, describing the parade, "and three Green Berets who marched mean and proud, but that was all there was from our war."

Both of the others snickered.

"There were some younger Gold Star mothers marching. Guess they want to show how proud they are their sons died for their country."

Again the two snickered.

"Why didn't you boys march?" Tim asked.

Again the snicker. Fred kept tugging at his shirt to hide the seamed pink scar that ran up from his back, under his right ear, and up his jaw to his eye.

"I do like the music," Will said with a horrible smile. "We had a colonel once, lost his whole unit, then, back at base, lined up their boots in formation and played Sousa marches." They both snickered.

"Well, today's a day for celebration in America, so what are you boys doing?" Tim clapped his hands on their backs. "I have an idea. Paula's got a couple of friends who are hot to trot, and we could get a cooler of beer and head down to the beach?"

"Yeah," said Fred. "Sounds great." And he snickered.

"Sure," Will said.

"We could get some Cuban sandwiches or a pizza. I'll give Paula a call." Tim picked a dime from his pile of money and turned toward the pay phone. Will's hand touched his.

"Loads of time," he said. "Don't rush it." And he snickered.

"Well, I don't know. Paula might be going out tonight, and the girls—let's see where we stand now."

"Finish your beer," Will said with a dour face.

"What the hell's the matter with you?"

"I don't like making plans so fast," Will said, and he turned to Fred and they both giggled.

Outside, the parade had ended and the street was filled with children carrying balloons and popsicles and hot dogs, and parents urging the children toward home, and drum majors and cheerleaders and prom queens and the grand marshal passing by the smoky glass.

"I'm getting antsy," Tim said. "I want to do something today."

"Hey, Rudy!" Will called to the bartender. Will pointed to Tim with his thumb. "Get him a beer and shut him up."

And the beer came, and Timothy drank it, and the sun set with no plans made, and they stayed until far into the night when the winos came in to spend the change they had panhandled. They sat in the purple glow of the television, drinking quietly, rarely uttering a word, drinking beer after beer as if the beers were mugs drawn from Lethe, the river of forgetting.

That snicker refined itself into an attitude toward life that frightened Timothy Murphy. He saw during his hangover the next morning how prone he was to the cynical shrug, to the giggle, how easily he might spend the rest of his life in a smoky bar, deadening the pain with cheap, warm beer. True, he hadn't been as badly wounded as they, and he hadn't the disability check to rely on, but he loathed self-pity. He saw their giggle as self-pity. They were simply committing a slow suicide, and that terrified him. Directly, it was that afternoon in the bar that caused Timothy Murphy to propose to Paula and to move to the other side of Miami where he knew no one.

As a result of that Memorial Day afternoon, Tim forged a steadfast rule never to talk about Viet Nam in bars. Surprised by Luke's straightforward manner, he recoiled from the discussion. Yet Luke was so easy-going. Luke talked freely about his time in-country. Luke seemed to accept the horror he'd seen and accomplished there. He filtered all the jagged, chaotic, gory events through his candor, drew out the kernel of humor in each anecdote, and held it above the horror and fear and misery of his tour of duty, as they got progressively drunker, for them both to admire and laugh at. He even drew Tim out about his days there, and five o'clock found them at a table with two empty beer pitchers, laughing energetically at one of Tim's stories.

"And we laughed," Tim said, fighting for control, "we laughed until we thought we were going to die. Here's a guy . . . oh, man!"

"Boy, that's army for you. That *is* army."

Again they laughed, and Tim drank more beer. Luke controlled himself. "Here's the army for you," he said, raising his index finger, struggling to get his breath. "It's Easter time and I'm still real green, right? We're expecting our hot meal in for the day. These guys run down to the slick when it comes in, and there's incoming shells all over. They drop the meal and some other crate there and they give us a box of, ah, Halloween costumes and decorations by mistake. You think these guys tossed them away? No way. They were out there on the LZ with bunting, and throwing streamers around, decorating." He laughed. "Jimi Hendrix blasting all over the place." He laughed, then took a deep breath. "I kept wondering what the VC was going to think about us, as if they really cared, like we were nuts or something."

Luke paused, then grew pensive. "You just couldn't help but dream about home, though. That's all I ever dreamed about, thinking to myself that, okay, someone just yell out, 'Time out. Start this dream over.' And I'd be in it. Home."

"Yeah," Tim agreed. "There wasn't anything to think about but to go home." And he stared into space as Luke rose to visit the men's room, and he remembered.

He remembered now the camaraderie of his fire team. They'd seen six firefights together and they'd come through unscathed. A strong bond was formed among them, the bond of men in combat, as if anything that happened to one of them happened to them all. He remembered their bravado, their devil-may-care posturing, the plans they'd make for the day when home would be a reality. He remembered the Badman, Eric Badowsky, son of a Pennsylvania coal-mining family, and the plans they'd made together, and he remembered Hartz, superstitious Hartz, who couldn't leave because he feared that stepping on the plane to get out would seal his fate and the plane would be shelled.

They had shared a bunker at Khe Sanh together with Rafer, a handsome black from east Los Angeles, and Sanchez from New York's Spanish Harlem. Monsoon season had arrived and water seemed to hang in midair in sheets. To ease the depression and to ignore the rain pelting on the metal of the quonset roof, they played rock'n'roll tapes loudly—Jimi Hendrix, the Rolling Stones, Jim Morrison and the Doors—music with a loud angry pulse and lewd, threatening lyrics that suited the mood.

"Hey, Badman," Rafer called from his bunk. He was lying back, reading a letter from home. "What you going to do when you get home?"

Tim Murphy raised his head, but Sanchez, sitting on his bunk fingering imaginary frets on an imaginary guitar, didn't look at them. Badman didn't answer at first.

"Man," Tim called protectively, "he's coming with me to Miami."

Badman perked up. "Shit yeah, man. Me and Tim are gonna buy ourselves a fucking boat and put together a charter fishing business—permanent R&R in the sun."

"Right on!" Tim cried in agreement. They slapped each other's hand to show their brotherhood.

"What the fuck do you know about boats?" Sanchez asked disgustedly. "You're from Pennsylvania!" Still his fingers played the imaginary guitar.

"Man," Tim answered for the Badman, "you don't have to know nothing about boats. You just gotta lay back at the controls and rake in the money from all those fat-cat Yankees that come on *dowwwn!*"

This excited Badman and he waved his hands in the air. Badman always wore black leather gloves with the fingers cut out, and he made a fist and pumped it in the air. "Whoa, yeah!"

Sanchez just shook his head in mock disgust. "Shit, I don't envy the Coast Guard or nothing. They're going to be busy as hell saving your balls everyday."

Badman flung up his middle finger to stop Sanchez from spoiling the dream.

"Hey," said Timothy Murphy to change the subject, "look at this." He showed Badman a picture that had just arrived in the mail, a picture of two young women. The older of the two was striking a sexy pose and the younger was jumping up in the air.

"One foxy lady, man," Badman said.

Tim smiled to himself with satisfaction. "Yeah, Renée is that, but I'll tell you though, her little sister is the one." He nodded and his eyes lit with excitement.

"She's got a sister?" Badman asked.

"Yeah, right there." Tim pointed to the little girl jumping in the air.

"There she is, right there. She writes to me more than Renée does. Paula. Boy! She really is something."

Just then a clap of thunder shook the bunker and the lights went out.

"Goddamned fucking generator again!" Rafer said in disgust. In the gloom Tim lit a joint the size of a cigar, and exploding seeds sent trails of flame like tracer bullets arching to his lap. "Shit!" He arose and walked toward the entrance, handing the joint to Rafer.

"Do-da-a!" Rafer said with pleasure.

Tim reached the entrance and gazed at the incessant rain and at a jet racing overhead. "When it rains like this," he said thoughtfully, "it reminds me of a spring day back home."

"Home," Rafer said and nodded. "Can't wait."

"Man," Sanchez said with excitement, "you know what I'm going to do when I get back to the world?"

Comically Rafer leaned over to him, rolled his eyes, and said in a deep voice, "Say, what?"

"Why, I'm going to go and I'm going to buy me a VW, man. I'm going to pick up my girl. Man, we're going to travel around the country. Chicago, San Francisco, Seattle, New York, Miami, New Orleans. You know, maybe someday I'll come visit you guys."

Badman liked the idea of Sanchez, an inner city Puerto Rican, traveling cross-country in a Volkswagen. He and Rafer leaned over Sanchez to ride him a bit.

"You hear that, Rafer, man?" Badman bared his teeth in a smile. "Goddamned 'Rican in a bug."

All of them laughed, except Sanchez, whose pride was hurt. "Hey, fuck you, Badman!"

"A Bug-a-Rican!" Rafer taunted him. Tim turned away.

"Tim, man," Sanchez appealed to him. "Why don't you tell these guys to cut it out?"

"Fuck you." Tim laughed. "You're a Bug-a-Rican."

And as they laughed, suddenly Hartz broke into the bunker, rain dripping from him onto Sanchez's bunk.

"Jesus, Hartz!" Sanchez cried.

Hartz fell on the floor. Badman approached him. Disappointment registered in all their faces because Hartz, who was supposed to be shipped out, had returned. This, in a strange way, seemed to lessen their own chances for reaching home.

"What happened, man?" Badman asked angrily. "I thought you'd be halfway to California by now."

"Slick got hit coming in this morning," Hartz explained. "Four of them bought the farm. They went and canceled all flights today, so here I am."

"Hey, Hartz!" Tim Murphy called. He talked angrily, sarcastically, as if he were having the discussion with himself. "You ever going to leave this country, or are you planning on being buried in this shit hole?"

Hartz seemed shamed.

"Bullshit, man!" Badman said, playing with his knife, terror in his eyes.

"Same old song," Sanchez said with a roll of his eyes.

Tim sat on the edge of his bunk and dropped his head between his hands in frustration. None of them, it seemed, would ever get out of there. Home, he thought, home. He looked around him now and noticed he was still in the Statue of Liberty Bar. Luke was returning from the men's room. Reliving those moments, poignantly now, for Luke's anecdotes brought them back to life, he remembered the aching feeling when he'd gone to sleep each night, the fear in that bunker that he would never see the sunrise, that he would never see Paula or home again. Now, here he was in the bar, drinking beer, calling up these buried memories. Home. Paula would be waiting for him, wondering if he'd found work. Paula, the young girl leaping high in that picture, so long ago in that bunker so far away. Now his wife of a decade, home, waiting.

"Another pitcher?" Luke asked, picking up an empty one.

"No, man," Timothy Murphy said, "I've got to get home."

But tonight, home with his family, it was different. Although the children quietly played a game and Paula riffled through the bills to see which ones were overdue, which could be postponed, and Tim read a newspaper, the peace and contentment of a previous evening wasn't there. Occasionally the words on the page of his newspaper blurred, or else jumped about uncontrollably. He remembered reading the falsified body counts out of stateside newspapers in his bunker. He remembered mocking the red, white, and blue reporting. He remembered a woman journalist from a Yankee newspaper who looked for patriotism, order, discipline, and progress, and found a hellish chaos she disdained.

Most of all, though, Tim remembered the television broadcasts of maimed GIs, of thatched villages, paddy dikes, the street urchins of Saigon, ARVN colonels and high-ranking Vietnamese politicians. Television coverage had changed the war. The blood, brutality, and explosive violence, the incendiary power of napalm and phosphorus grenades were broadcast nightly into American living rooms. Emotions ran high, the violence polarized the generations, and politicians at home, always looking for the most popular stand with

the voters, adopted indecision and duplicity as strate-
gies even with their generals in the field. And who
suffered? The men in the bush. They suffered from
waffling decisions and reversals from headquarters.
They suffered from the part-time nature of the war
fostered by the populace's negative reaction—each man
viewed his role not as part of a company or brigade,
but simply as an employee whose employment ended
on a specific date, when he returned home. And how
they suffered when they returned home—buses at the
San Francisco airport had been lined with chain-link
fence, because, when homecoming troops were transported from the planes, riots often broke out, with
baseball bats, bottles, and rotten fruit.

"Honey?" Paula said. "Hon?"

His train of thought broken, Tim grunted acknow-
ledgment.

"We got our third notice."

He continued to read the newspaper and discovered
he had been reading a story about the rising unemployment rate. "What third notice?"

"The TV people."

"What about it?" His voice held a note of annoyance.

"You said you were going to take care of it. Are
you?"

Timothy gritted his teeth, thrust his newspaper aside,
and to the astonishment of his children quietly playing
their game at the coffee table, sprang from his chair,
crossed to the television, and flicked it off. "There," he
said, returning. "It's taken care of."

"Hey!" Ellen protested. "I was watching that!"

"No you weren't. You were playing that game." Tim
sat back down and reached for his newspaper. Ellen
stood up defiantly and turned the television back on,

looking for her father's reaction. Again he sprang from his chair. This time he ripped the cord from the wall and flung it at Paula. "Here," he said sarcastically, "send that with the next payment."

In fear, Ronnie stood and ran from the room.

"Ellen," Paula said in an uneven voice, striving for control, "go see about Ronnie." Ellen looked with fear from her mother to her father. They were glaring mightily at each other. She, too, left the room. Paula stood up, holding out the cord to Tim. "Well," she said icily, "what was that stunt all about?"

He crumpled his paper together and thrust it aside. "I'm tired of hearing about that goddamned TV," he said through his teeth. His eyes burned with rage. "I'm tired of people fucking with me!"

"Oh, don't give me that," Paula said, discarding his explanation. Her eyes narrowed suspiciously. "I know there's something else bothering you. I just want to know what it is."

Tim pointed his finger threateningly at her. "Don't start with me, Paula. Don't start with me."

"I'm not. I don't want to fight," she pleaded. "I just want to know what is going on."

Fighting to control his anger, Timothy Murphy gripped the arms of the chair, pulled himself up, and brushed past her toward the door.

She turned, the cord hanging limply in her hand. "Where are you going, Tim?"

"Out!" he growled, slamming the door behind him. Paula stared at the door for a long moment after he had left. Then she turned, the cord limp in her hand, and looked at the blank television screen, trying to envision the turbulent scenes that were playing in Timothy's mind and memory.

He drove to escape. The slick night street soothed him. No, he didn't want to drink. He wanted to be alone in some cool place where he could breathe freely. Signal lights turning green, yellow, red, green, yellow, red seemed somehow to guide the path of his car. The pattern of streets, the ease of steering the car, of traveling upon impulse wherever he wanted to go, the pedestrians and the hookers and the cops he passed, the anonymity pleased him, and the order pleased him.

Yet something was wrong, something he did not want to face. He replayed the scene in his living room, and he knew it wasn't right. He knew he should have handled it differently, but he knew at the moment there had been no other course of action. No other course of action. He had to do what he had to do, and he had done what he had to do. No need for regrets. Regrets were useless. Guilt benefited no one. He must push on. Yet the faces of his children, their expression of panic—that bothered him. Paula, standing with the cord hanging limply, as if she wanted to remedy a situation but didn't know where to plug it in—that bothered him too. He owed her better than that. He knew he did. She had been too kind and understanding to treat that way. But could his pride admit his error?

Pride, he thought, easing his car into the right lane and driving along the beach. In the darkness the waves crashed and spilled and frothed upon the sand. Pride. What little he had left. Like the great groaning ocean his heart swelled and spilled over. Oh, he wanted to do the right thing, he wanted desperately to do the right thing. But how could he take the strong emotions that ebbed and flowed like the dark tide to his right, how could he put them into form and words and substance? It made no sense. He only wanted to live an ordinary anonymous life. He didn't want to be a hero or a genius or a tycoon. He only wanted to live unmolested, untroubled by things that he couldn't do anything about, doing the things he might control in the best possible way.

He turned back toward Miami. A great neon hoax, he thought. Thrusting toward the stars with arrogant skyscrapers, assailed by the ocean winds, offering sin and drugs and ten thousand immediate pleasures. Couldn't they see? Couldn't any of them see? The waterfront proudly faced the sea, but the grandeur and the wealth quickly trailed off to the north, inland, *in-country*, he laughed at the pun, trailing off into the Everglades.

The swamp, the lush green, teeming swamp that he remembered as a child. Like a jungle it lay festering, each day fostering life in green profusion, replete with danger and death to catch the unwary. Couldn't any of them see how the city clung to the edge of a continent, looking bravely out to sea, not daring to look back?

Meeting Luke troubled him. The insignia troubled him. There were always reminders. What had been Luke's experience there? How could he be so lackadaisical, so accepting? Every vet he'd ever met had that one moment, one memory heightened by combat hysteria that crystallized the whole experience. Didn't Luke have that one moment, like a dammed-up stream he couldn't get beyond, that caused the deep dark waters to swell and flood and threaten to burst? Of course he had. Everyone who had gone through 'Nam had, and though they tried to drink or screw or swallow drugs to deny it, they must from time to time come face-to-face with it.

Luke caused him to come face-to-face with it again He shrank from the confrontation. He preferred to remember the camaraderie, the good times for however good they were. Luke forced him to bring it all back to mind, because Luke was coping well. Luke never had moments like these.

Memories, memories. A hundred vignettes crowded in upon him: playing football on the landing zone at Khe Sanh before the siege was on and NVA mortars found the range to harry incoming craft and pockmark the strip so Seabees had to be summoned daily. Those were good days. How Rafer could run!

"I was scouted, man, offered scholarships to USC and Irvine." And his dazzling white teeth would flash. "Football was my life, man. Football and all that white pussy just dying, aching and squirming, man, to jump on a football hero. Man!" And he'd sigh and shake his head and smile regretfully. "I flunked my ass out first year, man. Only got one season in."

"Yeah," Badman would taunt him, "but there's hundreds of little chocolate-colored babies running around southern Cal looking for their daddy."

Those dark nights on patrol when the cold numbed them and they'd light a campfire from plastic explosive and talk about life, Tim cherished the memories. He enjoyed Sanchez's Spanish Harlem view of the American Dream.

"When I get back to the neighborhood," he'd say, "I'm going to be admired, man. My gang, man, my gang was the toughest around. Our turf was secure, man. No problem for women and kids to walk the streets. And they'll know then that I been through this, and I'm one mean motherfucker 'cause I survived this shit." Sanchez enjoyed street fighting, and though fairly useless in the jungle, he could read the alleys and doorways and rooftops of Vietnamese cities better than anyone in the platoon.

"Like shit they'll admire you," Badman would say. "Like shit." He laughed. "Others have taken over in your absence, man. You're here and they're there and you'll go back, one dumb sap for putting up with all this bullshit."

"You don't know nothing," Sanchez said. "My papa came from Puerto Rico. My people all came from Puerto Rico. Though we complain about the cops and the welfare stiffs, we love America. We believe in America. In America there's hope and opportunity. This is bad shit over here, but when I get back, I'll be respected. I'll be somebody."

And he looked with glazed eyes into the fire, toked on the joint, and passed it to Tim. Above all, though, there was Badman. Badman. A nickname fraught with the same irony as the slogans painted on helmets and flakjackets, and tried, like the slogans, to hide the raw innocence and youth of the soldiers—Attila the Hun, El Capitan, Rat Man, Johnny the Shiv, Tommy the Hitman, Eric the Badman. Badman. They first met when Tim arrived at Bravo Company, and they became fast friends. Innocent and gullible, Badman admired Tim for his worldliness, his resourcefulness, his courage. During a firefight in the Highlands, Badman's M-16 jammed and he was pinned down behind the massive roots of a banyan tree. It was Tim, heedless of his own safety and crazed with fear for Badman, lobbing grenades, who ran to his aid and succeeded in freeing him from the crossfire.

"You saved my life," Badman told him afterward on the Huey back to camp as the fear ebbed from their muscles. Badman had faced death that time, and had been deeply affected by the experience. "Tim, you saved my life. I will never forget that."

Thinking of that time he saved Badman, Tim grew weary of prowling the streets and highways. Yet he did not want to return home. He did not want to see others. He parked in the spacious lot of a shopping plaza, and he sat, his hands on the steering wheel, and he remembered. Badman laughed at all his jokes, sought his advice, imitated him. Tim enjoyed the role of older brother; it made him feel needed, made him feel his advice would indeed have a beneficial impact on Badman, would in turn protect Tim in the jungle war. He remembered Badman, drenched with rain, laughing in his poncho. He remembered him stripped to the waist, his dog tags flashing in the sun as he danced drunkenly in the sun hollering, "Charlie! Here I am, Charlie! Give me no sass, kiss my ass, ass, ass!"—spreading his arms in an embrace of the sun, of life, of the brotherhood forged by combat. Yes, Timothy Murphy was always drawing Badman back, reining in his impulsive nature, saving him from himself. "Get down! Get down, Badman! Charlie doesn't need a target!"

And he remembered the day of the mortar shelling when together they ran, lungs bursting, the sandbagged foxhole ahead promising safety, the shells closer behind them, then suddenly in front of them. Charlie's mortars corrected the range, an explosion empted so close it rattled their molars. They both dove and tumbled into the foxhole.

"Hey, man," Tim shouted as another explosion rocked the ground and Badman screamed. "Stay down here. Get down!" Tim pulled him to the ground, and they both curled up in the fetal position against the sandbags as another shell hit. Again Badman lifted his head.

"Stay down!" Tim insisted. "What's the matter with you?"

Another shell shook the ground. Badman screamed in fear, "Yiiiiiii!", his eyes impossibly wide.

"Oh, Christ!" Tim gasped. They huddled together again as the rain of steel and exploded earth fell around them.

"You okay?" Tim asked.

"Yeah, sure. Sure, I'm okay," Badman said, nodding. "Sure, I'm okay. I'll be okay."

Still Tim saw the raw fear in Badman's eyes. He wanted to comfort him. He considered how best to do it, then he said, "Man, you promise you won't laugh if I tell you something?"

Badman screamed as another shell shook the ground, then he fought mightily for control. "What is it?"

"I'm scared," Tim said. "I'm scared shitless."

Again the ground shook and the explosion deafened them. Tim looked at Badman and saw he was beginning to cry. This unnerved him. He wanted to hug the Badman, to cry together because he knew they were about to die. Charlie had found the range.

"Oh, yeah?" Badman asked. He fought back the tears. "Only if you want to, man, if it'll help you, man." He reached out his hand in the black glove with no fingers. "You can hold my hand, Tim." His hand in the glove was trembling when Tim clasped it tightly in his own. Tears ran down the Badman's face.

"It's okay, Badman. Everything is going to be all right."

And Badman smiled through his tears, then squeezed his eyes shut as another shell exploded.

*   *   *

Tim shook himself out of the reverie. He was alone in his car in a parking lot, a deserted parking lot lined into separate spaces that looked like long lines of railroad track. His was the only car beneath the glow of the fluorescent lamps. This, this was anonymity in American suburbia.

The boat he and Badman had planned to buy, only a pipe dream, Tim's pipe dream, shared with the Badman to suggest there would be a future after so much hell a future when things would take care of themselves. He would never buy a boat, Tim knew. He'd only been thinking of his uncle's fishing boat, out on the high seas, to help himself through. He'd allowed the Badman to share in his private glimpse of heaven—floating on the sea beneath the sun, far from land and all the petty, human squabbles generated by cities, together they'd float away from court suits and arguments and street fights and war, two men, happy and secure together, far from land and jungles and fear. And Badman had believed him, even wrote his father that after the war he was moving to Florida to buy a charter boat.

Tim came to see the boat fantasy was a farce, a cheat, like a lie to a child. He had watched the Badman grab on to the fantasy desperately, desperately wanting to be with Tim, to be happy and secure after the war. But there was no boat, no rich Yankees, no easy life in the sun. There was only heat and rain and mud and jungle and the ever-present fear, the tangible threat of Charlie lurking in the jungle. Life was cheap. That was the vision they came to see. That's what truly shocked the Americans, Timothy Murphy believed. Life was cheap and meaningless, but Americans wouldn't give up their illusion that there was something sacred about it.

The military strategists couldn't cope with the VC tactic of sending sappers up to the wire with explosives around their neck to breach the camp's protective wall. Just like the kamikazes of World War II. How could the VC value their own soldiers' lives so little? Himself and Badman, seeing dead civilians unburied for weeks, chewed by dogs, seeing women and children, a nine-year-old girl peddling herself for money to buy food, seeing that inscrutable look of the elderly that spoke volumes about human misery, how, they asked, could life be so expendable?

Badman had the eyes of sadness, of a sweet innocence cheated of its fondest hope and dream. But still he needed to believe that life indeed did make sense, and so Tim had dreamed up the boat. The lesson that life was cheap hit home, and few could cope with it in-country, and afterward, returning home. Leaving with notions of winning glory, of advancing democracy in a foreign land, of coming to the aid of their country, the soldiers saw that nothing mattered. All they saw was the cruel hoax of lying politicians, as massacres and double crosses multiplied, the cruel hoax that their lives, once precious and worthy, full of promise, their lives didn't matter to anyone. They were bullet-meat, cannon fodder. Their existence was meaningless, their presence in-country absurd.

Tim had been drinking beer one afternoon when a gung-ho vet was discussing matters with a redneck owner of an orange grove.

"I've got gook metal in my arm," the vet said proudly.

"That's right," the grove owner, Mr. Edwards, said.

"I got shot in World War II, and I'm proud of my Purple Heart. These student fucks, carrying signs and burning their draft cards, they should take the little faggots over and dump them in 'Nam and let them see what it's like."

"I got gook metal in my arm," the vet said proudly again. He operated a tow truck and collected junk cars.

"I don't understand these kids!" Mr. Edwards said. "You went, Bob, and your brothers went, and you lost a cousin, poor Billy. And these lousy little queers."

The bartender had hair halfway down his back and a beard and an earring. Neither Mr. Edwards nor Bob Wooter knew he had been in the Tet Offensive. They were addressing some of their frustration his way. He noticed, and tried to ignore them.

"I got gook metal." Bob pointed to his arm.

"Hey," JT, the bartender, said, "what are you boys going to eat for dinner tonight?"

"What?" Edwards asked. "I haven't thought of it, why?"

"Just tell me. Burgers? Pizza? What?"

"I figured I'd get a Cuban sandwich," Bob said.

"I think 'The Queen' is preparing pork chops," Mr. Edwards said. He called his wife "The Queen," and the irony was lost on no one.

"Well, you're having a Cuban sandwich, and you're having pork chops. What do you think your senators are eating tonight? Lobster? Steak? Fine French wines? And they got nice little secretaries to enjoy for dessert, and fine cigars. And you're here, drinking beer from Peter's filthy lines, warm beer, and you'll be going home to your wives. And these bastards in Washington are keeping the war going over there so you

can lose a cousin, and maybe a son, and they're dining
in splendor and the boys are out in the bush. Doesn't
that bother you?"

"But, but I got gook metal in my arm!" Bob protested.

And JT laughed. "Yeah, you do, and they don't."

"Ah," Mr. Edwards growled, "the kid's right." And
his frown was one of impossible dismay. "Those bastards! Ah, what does it matter, anyway?"

"It matters," JT said, "because they're having fun
and our boys are dying."

"Ah," Mr. Edwards said, "let's just get drunk and
piss on it."

And Tim had laughed and laughed at their realization of the great hoax. And now? As if wounds that
had been scarred over were now bleeding afresh, Timothy Murphy recognized the emotion that he thought
he'd lost forever—the protective intimacy he had felt
toward Badman. He could feel that emotion, that close-
ness with another man who'd been through battles
and who understood what he himself knew, and he
tried to deny it. But Luke had been through it all.
Somehow Luke rekindled in him that old feeling. Even
though Luke seemed happy-go-lucky, Tim could feel
the hurt lurking there, and he wanted to shield him
from it. Luke talked candidly about his experience
there, but Luke needed him.

Should he get involved? That was the big question
on Tim's mind. Why? What would he get out of it
besides another possible hurt as bad or even worse,
worse than the first. Could he gamble that soldiering
could be a foundation for a friendship in civilian
life? Could he risk the endless discussion of 'Nam,
and all the long-buried memories brought up again
and again?

He felt an affinity for Luke, and a friendship developing strongly, quickly, undeniably, and this is what he both feared and longed for. He wanted to control his emotions. He needed to steer a path to avoid the awful hurt. Opening up to Luke as he had that afternoon made him vulnerable. Should he continue to do so? Luke had made plans to meet him the next afternoon, to hunt for jobs together, and Tim nodded, started his car, pulled out of the empty parking lot. He owed Paula some explanation, and he knew that he would meet Luke the next day. And he thrust his thumb into the air. "Thumbs up." And he nodded, congratulating the human heart on its stupidity, for no matter how severe the pestilence, how deep the soil is salted with tears, one seed of hope will send up its shoot, and the shoot, with colossal, frightening arrogance, will tremble and threaten to bloom.

Chapter 4

Luke and Tim became fast friends. Both still unemployed, they used their job searching as a pretext to be together. In common they held the unholy experiences of warfare and death and destruction, but they did not view 'Nam as a disgrace that they had to hide from each other. No. For them it had been a baptism by fire. They had passed through the ordeal, had been subjected to intense heat and pressure, and as ordinary gray limestone becomes startlingly white marble, so, too, had they been changed. Now they had found a new innocence. Together they could act like boys. Together they could joke and play and mock things, safe in the reaction of the other.

Each morning they met at a street corner. From there they made calls and set up appointments for interviews, then accompanied each other to the various firms and plants, encouraging each other about

what to say, then calming each other when the inter
view turned out poorly.

They clowned in diners, on buses when their cars
were being repaired; they gave directions, flirted with
girls, ambled along the beach, shared beers and sodas,
and they talked. After they had been together for two
weeks, Luke revealed that he was an artist. He painted,
dabbled in sculpture, and had dreamed for a time
about devoting his life to art. He had dreamed about
striking it rich with his artworks. Tim, of course,
recognized the veteran's syndrome—a need, after the
hell of 'Nam, to have things fall into place, to be
okay for now and forever, to take care of themselves
automatically. He and Badman had shared the fantasy
of owning a pleasure boat. Tim smiled when Luke
told him about the art world, yet he said nothing.
They were walking along a busy street toward an
interview for Luke, and Luke was trying to find
something to say to his prospective employer.

"My old lady, man, she flipped out at some of the
shit I painted and put together." Luke laughed. "She
said I didn't live in reality. That I should forget the
past, let it die in peace. Man," Luke groaned, "she
wanted me to take a job as a clerk in her cousin's
department store! No way! That ain't my style."

"So, what happened?"

"When I refused, she walked. She said she had to
think things out and she asked me to split for a while.
So I found this pad." His voice grew nasal and thin,
ringing with insincerity. He shrugged. "It's all right.
It's fine. No, actually it's great having no strings at-
tached, being free for a while. I can get all the bimbos
I want and bring them home, and she can't say a
word."

"That'd be the life," Tim lied.

"Yeah." Luke paused. "I haven't done much in that direction, though." He laughed shallowly. He looked down. "Wonder if everything still works right. Quite a blow to your ego when your old lady throws you out . . . but, boy! What's that?" Luke had spied a cluster of naked mannequins, standing by a department store, and he had a pressing desire to change the subject. "Life and art merge at last!" he cried, and he embraced a bald, naked female mannequin. "I'm in love, Timothy!" he cried in boyish enthusiasm. "I'm in love!"

Tim laughed. "Are you asking her out?"

"No, man!" Luke said in mock disdain. "I'm taking her home straight off!" And he seized the mannequin and darted around the corner with it. Tim looked both ways to see if anyone had seen the theft, then he ran, laughing, after Luke.

Luke had just purchased a threadbare sofa for the studio apartment he rented. Instead of looking for work one afternoon, he and Tim transported the sofa to his apartment and lugged it up a flight of stairs. Upon entering, Tim scanned the walls and saw lurid canvases of shocking shapes and colors. They deposited the couch heavily upon the floor, and Tim groaned, straightened out his back, and looked at the various amateurish paintings.

"So, this is your art," he said noncommittally.

"This is definitely 'Early Lukian'!" Luke said in self-mockery. He waved his hand at the paintings—a geometric design in blood red and metallic blue, a white and black painting suggesting both an embryo and a skeleton, a green creation with the eyes of beasts peering out from under leaves shaped like a peacock's fan.

"Some weird shit, man," Tim said.

Luke looked around the room. "It is weird shit," he said. Tim scanned the walls, the lack of furniture, of comforts, mentally contrasting this apartment with the home he had filled with furniture and his children's toys. His eye caught a frame, and examining it, he saw combat medals.

"Whoa! Look at this!" He pointed to the glass and enumerated the medals. "A silver star, bronze star. Two bronze stars with valor. A Purple Heart and an air medal." He looked up, impressed, but with a tinge of irony. "We got a real fucking hero!"

"Up yours, too," Luke said. He was slightly embarrassed by the display. "Won't buy a cup of coffee."

"Yeah," Tim agreed. "Nice frame, though."

"You still got yours?" Luke asked. It had become something of a boasting contest now, to see who was more humble, or more bitter.

"Uh . . . no," Timothy said lamely. "I must've lost them or something." Tim turned away from Luke and sought shelter on the couch they had just carried up.

Now Luke was very embarrassed. "Well, uh, my wife, she just wanted me to keep them for the kid, so she put them in this thing. She kind of made it, you know?" He shrugged, looked to change the subject, and saw his photo album. "I've even got some of my pictures still." He tossed it at Tim. "Catch."

As Tim caught the book a pamphlet fell out. He picked it up and examined it. It was a pamphlet from the vet center.

"Vet center?" he asked Luke, looking up.

"Yeah, well, they, uh, they kind of helped me one time." Luke shrugged and turned away as if he didn't want to talk about it. Tim believed only losers went to the vet center. He thought of it as an afternoon tea party where men talked of their hard times far away and long ago, and they sank into each other's welcoming pity as if into a hot tub. He examined the pamphlet. And yet he had heard they never turned anyone away. They never laughed or criticized or pointed fingers of blame, and they never turned anyone away.

"What for?" Tim asked. He scrutinized Luke and saw something was the matter.

Luke made light of it. "Helped me find a job once . . . then, uh, I went down to help out with some of the guys who . . . who were a mess." He looked at Tim. His eyes narrowed. "They just had to talk. You know? They just had to get it out." He shrugged. "They *liked* to talk, to . . . rap. They got to rap."

Luke felt terribly embarrassed while Tim looked at the pictures. He went to fetch some beer. Tim hadn't responded, but he knew. It was shadowboxing they were doing, shadowboxing with each other. Each knew the horror glimpsed by the other, and now Luke had artlessly displayed his inability to cope with his personal share.

As Luke popped open a beer can and handed it to him, Tim looked up, scowling. He closed the album. His words weren't impatient, but they held a note of rebuke. "Having all this shit around, doesn't it make you . . ." He realized the implicit criticism, then softened the statement. "Damn! I just want to forget about it." He took the can of beer, sucked hard at it, and looked uneasily at the frame and the medals. He sighed mightily, then turned to sum up his opinion.

"Viet—fucking—Nam. What a fucking jerkoff!"

Luke looked relieved. Tim was letting him off the hook. He wouldn't have to explain anything now, and they could reenter this moment, his apartment, and the fact they were together now, so many years later.

"Yeah, well, that's pretty specific." He held up his beer. "I'll drink to that."

And Tim held up his beer as if to toast him. They raised their beer cans, then took a long swallow. That ended that.

The moment of examining the past was gone. Luke reached over and pulled out a picture and handed it to Tim Murphy. "Just check this out."

Tim looked at the picture and smiled. "Who's the good-looking kid?"

Luke reached proudly for the picture book. "Come on, that's my boy. Christopher."

Tim nodded. "Nice." He looked at Luke as if to say, I know how proud you must be. "Real nice, man."

"Thanks," Luke said, grimacing with regret. "Yeah, he's just great."

"Do you," Tim asked, "do you think you can work things out?"

Luke smiled and nodded. "Oh, yeah." He nodded again. "Our separation was a big mistake, big mistake." He looked sheepishly at Tim. He tried to explain because he knew Tim knew how difficult it was. "Everything was so crazy. But now we've been able to talk it all out, and . . . well, we've been seeing a lot of each other." He looked fondly at the picture, then he closed his eyes. "He's really something else. Christopher. You should see his curveball. He's already pitching. The kid's a natural." Luke looked at Tim. "Hey, you know what we got to do sometime? Get yours and mine . . ."

Tim smiled. "Yeah, it would be great." Another dream, of children playing over the graves and blood and tears. Tim nodded. "That would be great."

And Luke, satisfied that his wish was shared, leaned back and took a long swallow of beer.

Chapter 5

Godfather? Tim was someone to ask, some example. He agreed to "stand up" for the baby, but his heart wasn't in it. He owed it to Linda and Richie, but he didn't want to do it. He didn't want to preach, or—or to be responsible. He shied away from that. The baby had come a month before. The late-night call from the hospital, and the weeping and the laughter and the plans. Linda and Richie summoned Paula and Tim to the hospital. It was like before, the joy of new life, when Ellen and Ronnie had been born. Paula and Tim were wanted at the hospital to share the joy.

"Oh, my God," Richard cried to Tim, hugging him uncontrollably, "he's so beautiful! I can't believe it, Tim! I'm such a lucky man!" And the new life was bundled away before their eyes. Richie and Linda had tried unsuccessfully for five years to have a child, and so their joy was doubled. "Will you stand up for him?"

Richie asked. "Will you be Billy's godfather?" Tim
shrugged, "Sure, man, sure." Tim, though, though
deep and hard and long about that. He saw in his
growing children new hope for the world. They were
innocence personified and he hoped, he prayed, he lay
awake at night planning how he would ensure that
they would become experienced without being cor-
rupted. The line was a fine one and easily crossed.
Experience tempered the mind and heart and will
made it stronger, more resilient. Corruption debased
the mind and heart and will. Like a disease, corruption decayed the personality from within with guilt
and shame and self-loathing.

Tim had seen it so many times. Having crossed the
line only once, certain sensitive natures could never
go back. They tried to deny it, burn and scar it out of
their memory, but their efforts were like wild beasts
thrashing vainly in a net. They drugged and drank
themselves into a specious comfort, anesthetizing the
pain they themselves had created. They wandered
about, preaching how absurd or existential or damned
the world was, yet all the time they harbored a secret
hope that the world did make sense, that there was
meaning and everything would be all right. Yes, Timothy Murphy wanted to spare his children the ugli-
ness and the strife and the corruption. Taking on this
new responsibility, though, bothered him. He was answerable for his own actions—though to be sure, certain things he did brought him shame and doubt—and
for the upbringing of his own children, but serving as
godfather? That just might be expanding the circle a
bit too far.

Timothy Murphy was an Irish Catholic born and
bred, but he rarely practiced his faith. Irish Catholicism conferred both ethnic and religious burdens, even

n the laid-back eighties, burdens he chose not to shoulder. His mother's family, the Ryans, had been driven from the lush Emerald Isle by the great potato famine, sick of land-clearings and the tyranny of British absentee landlords. His father's father had escaped from the Black and Tans, British military thugs who harried Ireland after the First World War. Tim had believed all Americans were exiles, one way or another, and the Celtic stigma allowed Murphy the Mick to identify with Rafer the Nigger, Badowsky the Polack, and Sanchez the Spick. He had begun and lived his life on the outside looking in.

The Catholic religion had comforted him as a child. Some things were mysteries, indeed, so let them be mysteries. Let blind faith overcome all obstacles. Genuflect, bow, beat our communal breast. Confess our flaws and shortcomings. Accept the forgiveness and rise, like Christ on Easter Sunday, to a new life, redeemed. Forgiveness, that was what the church offered then, and what he didn't need now. He didn't need forgiveness because he had done nothing wrong. Didn't need forgiveness because the hell he'd been through made ordinary sins seem like a Sunday picnic. He didn't need forgiveness because the church couldn't offer it. The church had supported the war and so underwrote all the hell and the murder and the maimings. No, that wasn't right, Tim told himself, the church didn't support the war, that was too strong, but the church had adopted at times a hawkish attitude. An archbishop urging the men to spread democracy. Sure. Spreading democracy in that land with napalm and strafing was like spreading love around by raping women. It had been comforting to him as a child to believe. He wanted Paula and Ellen and Ronnie all to believe. But he couldn't anymore. Yet for the sake of

Linda and Richie, for the sake of their son, he fel
compelled to don a pious demeanor as mechanically a
he donned his suit and tie, and approach the baptis
mal font.

It was a happy day. Relatives, well-wishers, friends
and neighbors clustered in the warm glow of sunligh
through stained glass. The echoing voice of the pries
solemnly sanctified the moment. The baby in his bap
tismal gown looked so terribly weak and helpless, so
pink and wrinkled. Timothy Murphy swallowed hard
as the ceremony began.

"We are happy to present our child to be baptized,'
Linda said. She held the baby as Tim and Emily, the
godmother, stood by.

In a white stole and white vestments the elderly
priest turned his head to the mother. "You have asked
to have your child baptized. In doing so, you accept
the responsibility of training him in the practice of
the faith."

The baby began to cry and Tim's collar suddenly
felt a bit tight. Was he a hypocrite? Why hadn't he
refused? Couldn't he live up to any principles, even
nihilistic ones?

"It will be your duty," the priest continued to the
parents, "to bring him up to keep the God's command-
ments, as Christ says, by loving God and our neigh-
bor." The baby wailed still louder. "Do you clearly
understand what you are undertaking?"

"We do," the parents said solemnly.

"Are you ready to help the parents of this child in
their duty as good Christian parents?" the priest asked
the godparents.

"We do," Tim and Emily said together.

The crying grew louder and still louder. Tim winced.
Its echoes pierced him, made him want to place his

hands over his ears and scream. His sport coat, his tie, his combed hair, the front he presented here lacked sincerity and substance. He was a paper cutout of himself. And the baby was very much alive.

"Do you reject Satan, the Father of Sin and the Prince of Darkness?" the priest asked. Like a slithering snake, a bead of sweat trickled down Timothy Murphy's spine. He shivered and grimaced again. Sweat broke out upon his forehead. Satan.

Tim nodded. "We do," he and Emily said in unison. Satan. The Prince of Darkness. The word is out, man. Charlie's coming tonight. The raw fear of that one phrase! Grown men crying themselves to sleep. Charlie's at the wire. The Prince of Darkness. Violent explosions and oblivion. A message on a flakjacket—"Though I walk through the Valley of Death, I will fear no evil. I'm the meanest sum'bitch in the Valley"—and the kid, no more than seventeen, an unconsummated wish. Yet all around at night, the seething, steamy jungle, Charlie in his black pajamas.

"Do you believe in God, the Father of Light and Creator of Heaven and Earth?"

"We do," they said as the baby wailed, red-faced, a vein rising in its bald little forehead.

Tim lifted a small candle to light it from the Paschal candle. Easter. Life redeemed. Baptism. Closer he held the candle to the Easter flame, closer and closer until he heard the baby crying and the hootch exploding and the flames, the oily black smoke and the huge flakes of soot.

Tim shook his head. His throat was impossibly dry. "Parents and godparents," the priest said, "this light is entrusted to you to be kept burning brightly. This child of yours has been relightened to Christ." The candle in Tim's hand was lit and trembling. He turned to Emily, handed her the candle, and turned away from the others. Quickly and quietly he made his way through the vestibule and out of the hushed colored light of the church into the sun.

He thrust his hands into his pockets and kicked at a stone. He leaned against the church railing. It was wrong, all wrong. He should never have agreed to do it. Rather be a miserable son of a bitch to a friend than a hypocrite. Bullshit, bullshit, bullshit. Religion was bullshit, he believed, and the season of his own loss of faith returned.

In boot camp, a raw recruit, Timothy Murphy murmured the "Hail Mary" to bring on sleep each night. He had never been particularly religious before, but the subliminal comfort the "Hail Mary" gave him each night eased him into sleep, allowed him to feel secure. Someone was watching over him. Through his tour of duty, initially, he had confronted so much death and mutilation, he had seen so much blood and bone and had smelled so much rotting flesh that frequently he'd sought solace with the Catholic chaplain. As he confessed his sins, he felt the serenity of a clear conscience. Death was so near at hand, so imminent and pervasive that Tim wanted somehow to be on good terms with his past and with his Maker.

It was after he had heard an archbishop deliver a rousing address to assembled GIs. The hawkish posturing, the sense of a white man's burden here in an ancient and primitive land, the blatant warmongering severely shook his trust in Catholicism that day. Timothy Murphy questioned why the church should be pushing harder to escalate the war. Of course the atheism of Communism was anathema, but this war reached wider, this intrusion by America into an Oriental land reached deeper than religious dogma.

During many patrols, Tim had seen the rotting remnants of French colonialism: churches with pockmarked walls, convents with Sisters of Charity in winged bonnets, French orphanages and missions still striving to keep a faith alive after the political support of France had caved in. If they couldn't cling to a faith in the face of such upheaval, what then? Throughout the stricken, war-torn land he had seen vestiges of Catholicism. But what good had it done? Slowly Tim came to perceive a rotten feudal hold over this land that had been exploded by war.

It all crystallized for Tim late one morning while they were on patrol. A funeral procession moved along a paddy dike, an ordered procession, the crucifix, candles, acolytes, and mourners wending their way along the dike under pink clouds, and it had moved him. The sanctity of the procession seemed oddly fitting in this ancient land, fitting until the shell exploded.

It was a stray mortar shell. With no warning the dike, the procession, the casket, all exploded, and when he picked up his head after the ground stopped shaking, limbs and pieces of flesh lay strewn all about. The corpse had been thrown from the casket. It was the body of a young woman. She had been flung two hundred feet, and her left leg had been severed. She was the lucky one, though, for she was the one who had nothing to lose. Timothy Murphy looked upon this scene in utter horror. So full of death, this land would not allow its living to bury its dead.

A litany composed itself in his mind:

> Procession of twelve mourners—
> —Proceed at your own peril.
> Candle to the sunlight—
> —Light our faith, O Lord!

Valley of the rice fields—
  —Give us today our bread.
Woman of our valley—
  —May she rest in peace at last.
Rain of lead and fire—
  —Forgive us, Lord, we pray!

It was an American mortar shell. No one explained it. A few of the goggle-eyed bright boys from Intelligence showed up with clipboards and jotted down some things. But that was all. That was all. Some genius had misread his instructions. That was all.

And then the communal absolution the next day before the offensive began. They bowed and genuflected while the priest sprayed holy water over the five hundred assembled.

"Forgive us, O Lord, for the sins we have committed by thought, word, and deed." And Timothy Murphy glared up at the priest. He did not want forgiveness. He did not need forgiveness. The government had sent him in, ordered him to do these things. He didn't feel responsible. Forgiveness? He only wanted to be away from there, away from the death and maiming, the screaming and blood. It was on the offensive that he came to believe religion thrived upon warfare. "God" was on both sides, so they were both losers? The illogic was so blatant! It was then, during the offensive, that he stopped believing, and from that moment he stopped seeking forgiveness. He lost all hope and any sense that a deeper purpose supported what he did. He looked out upon the insanity with sullen, world-weary eyes and believed religion a superficial and inadequate explanation, designed to help the gullible cope. He did not consider himself gullible anymore. He simply wanted to be left alone.

Timothy Murphy had no strong reaction to Catholicism after that, only a profound indifference. A family, burying its daughter, its wife and mother, had been slain enacting the ritual. Just another coincidence in a jolly old land. Too many coincidences, too much death, and too much chance. Charlie wasn't Satan, he was only Charlie. Though he appeared and vanished like a spirit from the jungle, the mythology that cast Charlie as a demon blinded the entire American side to his true nature—guerrilla warriors fighting for their homeland.

Tim wasn't bitter or angry. He had just found the Chrstian explanation insufficient. Nor did he replace it with any other faith. He simply ignored what he deemed an extraneous elaboration on the facts of life and he chose to react only to what he could see and smell and hear and touch. And this new way helped.

They were herding the locals to the farther edge of the jungle so they might inspect the hootches for VC. A child of five or six came running from a hootch with a live grenade. Teddy had his back to the kid. Tim saw what was about to happen and instinctively fired. The child's naked body rose up, still running, and the grenade flew out of his hand into the crowd of locals. The explosion killed Teddy and six civilians.

For an entire night Tim pondered what was cause and what was effect. By trying to prevent Teddy's death, had he truly caused it? But that was before the incident with Badman. With Teddy's death Tim realized that there were no causes and no effects. Things just happened. That was all. There were burning bushes, burning hootches, whole jungles burning under the lick of napalm, but there was no voice of the Lord. There was no need for forgiveness since things just happened. Human agency was a joke.

Paula was at his side now. "What happened?" she asked, concerned.

"I don't know, uh, I don't know," Tim said, attempting to seem nonchalant. "It just got on my nerves." He shrugged. "It was so hot in there, you know?"

"Wasn't that hot," Paula said, then she looked suspicious. "Tim, is something wrong?"

"Yes," he snapped, "something is wrong." Then he tried to hide his misgivings. "I just don't feel good, okay?"

"Fine," she said, throwing up her hands in frustration. "Sorry!" she said sarcastically, and she started to back away.

"I'm sorry. I'm sorry," Tim said, realizing he had been too abrupt and defensive. Forgiveness. Apology. He didn't need it, but he did not want Paula to go back in angry. "Look, I don't know. It just got on my nerves," he tried to explain. "The baby crying, and everything. I guess, I kind of messed things up, huh?"

Tim placed his arms around her for support, and she smiled. "No, no you didn't. Honey, it was just a baby crying. You know, you've heard babies crying before."

"I know," Tim said sheepishly.

"I just want you to be honest with me, Tim," she said insistently. "I want to help you, and if you don't tell me what's on your mind, I can't help."

"I'm all right," he said with more confidence than he felt. "I just haven't been feeling very good. Maybe I'm catching Ronnie's bug."

Paula nodded, not believing the excuse was physical. They hugged and kissed and turned to reenter the church and to offer congratulations to the parents of Christ's newest Christian.

Chapter 6

For a long time Paula had told Tim he needed a friend. In his heart Tim had believed she was right, but he didn't want to admit it. A friend, another man to share the joys and the sorrows, to share his unique perspective upon the world, to call to go have a beer, or to help him fix the roof, or to go to a ballgame, watch girls, or play one-on-one basketball, a friend. It wasn't that family life with Paula was insufficient. He believed that with her and the children he had forged a self-sufficient family unit. But he wanted something more. He had had a friend once long ago, but things didn't work out. Yet now, with Luke, those old stirrings returned. Because Luke understood him, Luke read his mind and knew what he was thinking almost before he knew. Luke was ready with the right joke almost before the right occasion for the joke arose. Luke knew life from the underside, from 'Nam, yet was not bitter. In fact, Tim believed Luke coped far better with the memories of horror than he did.

At first he was reluctant, suspicious. He didn't want to be shaken from his torpor, and his gray, colorless afternoons. His simple desire to curl up with his wife and babies, to face the world as an adversary, overcame his better sense. He was scared. Yet Luke wanted nothing from him. Luke did not want to touch the deep-seated memories, to probe and hold his particular brand of human horror up to the light. Luke had an annoying habit, though, of bringing up the war often and without warning.

At first Tim ran Luke's motives through tests—drugs, women, voyeurism, money, crying towels—and none of them applied. What did he want, Tim kept asking himself. What did he want and why? Then Tim came to see that Luke wanted nothing at all, nothing Tim could get for him. He wanted only to be close and to share. When Tim found this out, he was delighted. His heart awoke. No longer did he need to carry the world upon his shoulders alone and look dourly to the future and plan his children's fate. Life could be fun, life *was* fun. Tim then felt bad about his suspicions, about his testing of Luke's motives. Yet Luke never seemed to notice. If he did notice, and Tim believed he did, it didn't matter.

Still they were unemployed. It had been three weeks. A few nibbles but no bites. One afternoon they passed the athletic field of a public school and Luke suggested they sit in the bleachers and eat the sandwiches Paula had made for them. Tim bought some Cokes, and they climbed into the bleachers to look down upon the playing field and read the want ads.

Tim was going through the ads to set an interview up for the afternoon when Luke said: "Look at how green that football field is." Tim knew something more was coming. "Reminds me of 'Nam." Tim winced. It seemed to spoil things for the moment. If one thing about Luke annoyed him, it was talking about before. "Boy, all they had was rocks and no grass when I played on it." Tim bit into his sandwich, and his imagination raced. He knew instinctively what was coming.

"You know what my first impression of 'Nam was?" Luke asked. "That I'd never seen anything so *green.*" He elbowed Tim, but Tim didn't want to talk about Nam. Tim buried his face in the newspaper ads.

"You played ball?" Tim asked, as if off the cuff.

"Yeah, sure," Luke said. He saw Tim's tactic and didn't want to intrude with details about 'Nam. He pointed down at the field, wanting to discuss what he himself had found valuable and true in his innocent high school days, but he looked over and found Tim engrossed in the newspaper.

But Tim was not engrossed in the newspaper. His mind and his memory galloped. The first view of 'Nam stuck with you. For Tim it was out of the window of a troop transport at sunrise on a cloudy morning. They had been flying high above the cloud cover in the radiant sunlight until the plane dipped and the cabin darkened as they entered the clouds, then out of the cloud cover and into the long gray day below. He saw only slums and bars then until the transport lifted him northward. Then the greens, the endless shades of green. The majestic countryside, as if carved in jade and emerald, beckoned him into its web, as though it was primal and eternal, above change or death. It seemed like some fertile, green, elemental dream to him. The villagers in their conical straw hats driving lazy water buffalo into the fields in wide wooden yokes.

The rice, slim filaments of rice peeking above the carefully guarded water level of each paddy, the hootches in a cluster, the aged patriarchs, wise as Solomon, and the women chewing betel nut. It was an eternal land, a land that would only suffer and change for the moment when American guns and computers and radios were present, but that would revert shortly afterward, as it had so many times before, to the Stone Age.

"Come on, man." Luke nudged him. "We better get some work or we can both go on welfare together."

"That's not funny, man," Tim said.

"I know it's not." Luke jostled him. "But you've got to lighten up."

"I can't afford to lighten up," Tim said moodily. He wanted, as he had wanted for the year he was in-country, to cling to this primal and pure view of the land. Yet it was always snatched away from him.

"Give me fifty cents," Luke said, "and I'll go and make some calls."

To appease him Tim searched in his pocket and pulled out a dollar. "Here," he said, "Paula gave me a dollar. You can have half."

"All I want is half," Luke said. "And give me the number down by the airport."

Tim scanned the paper for the number as Luke hopped down the stands seat by seat. "It's 765-9854," he called after Luke. "Let's get lucky this time!"

Luke flashed him a thumbs-up sign and jogged toward the concession stand and phone booth.

Nassau had been a good dream Tim and Paula shared, but it was a dream that wouldn't come true, at least not yet. Money was just too tight. Time away from town, in addition to the expense, would be time away from the "Great Job Hunt," as Luke dubbed it.

When they had discussed canceling the trip, Paula eemed cheerful and accepting. "We'll do it next year vhen everything is all right," she said hopefully.

There was no reason to pretend everything was fine or a few days, only to return to town and find that hings, indeed, were worse.

Tim didn't mind missing the trip, and this surprised im. When he bought the tickets, he wanted to get away with Paula. He wanted to talk and stroll along he beach and to have dinner out and make long, passionate love with her in the hotel room. He still wanted that, but not as intensely. He thought about it, and he could only theorize that his friendship with Luke had filled some vacancy, satisfied some impulse, and so he didn't need to escape and be alone with Paula, he didn't need to retrench.

The afternoon Paula returned the tickets to the travel agent, she was lost in thought about Tim. The money she folded into her purse would be welcome to pay bills. She was startled when she heard her name called. "Paula?" It was Linda Cummings. "Hi, how are you doing?"

"Oh, fine," Paula said wistfully. She nodded and attempted a smile.

"Have you got time to get a bite or something?"

"Sure."

As they walked, Linda chattered on about her new job selling real estate and what a difference it made in her relationship with her husband. Paula only half listened. As they waited to be seated at the restaurant, Linda noticed her silence and her self-absorption. When finally they did sit down and spread napkins in their laps, Linda asked, "What's troubling you, Paula?"

Paula smiled weakly. "Oh, nothing." She scanned the menu. "What's good here?"

Linda reached out and gently touched her hand. "I know there's something going on behind that pretty smile," she said playfully. "Tell me."

"Oh, it's Tim. It's been ten weeks he's been unemployed, and I'm worried." She looked up sadly. "It's tough finding work. No one's hiring and of course he wants something that will last so he won't have to go through this again."

"We went through the very same thing last year," Linda said sympathetically. "That's when I decided to get my broker's license."

"It affects men oddly," Paula mused. The waitress came and they both ordered salads and iced tea. She folded the menu and placed it back with the others. "It muffles or suffocates their ego so they can't function, they get very down on themselves, and they can't . . ." She smiled when she realized what she had said. "Oh, don't get me wrong on that score. Tim functions exceedingly well on that score, but it's the day-to-day, the morning-to-night functioning that is so hard. He has a terrible self-image, and he feels such awful guilt. I try my best to help him through it, but he holds himself responsible for the most bizarre things."

"When Mark was unemployed last year," Linda said, "he used to pick fights with me over the most petty things. Then, if I took the bait, he'd rail and fume at me. I soon learned what was up with him, and when he'd try to engage me in an argument, I'd be all sugary and smiles." She laughed. "Men can be such little boys."

"But there's something terribly deep-seated in Tim, some tremendous powerful feeling that things aren't as they should be and that he's somehow to blame." Again she smiled faintly. The waitress brought their drinks. "Well, you know."

"It's probably temporary," Linda offered with hope. "I'm sure as soon as he gets a job he'll be fine." She snapped her fingers. "He'll snap right out of it."

"God," Paula said, "I hope you're right." She thought a moment. Did Linda want to listen anymore? She looked up at Linda, considering, then she spoke: "Listen, I've got to tell you something, okay?" Linda nodded and knit her brow, wondering what it was that had been secret. "See," Paula said hesitantly, "it's not just this time. I mean, it's happened before."

"What has?" Linda asked, concerned.

"I remember when we first starting dating"—she smiled at the pleasant memory—"we'd be like laying out at the park . . . making out . . . and all of that. Any little noise . . . I mean *anything,* he would jump." Paula sipped her iced tea. "And then, right after we got married, he'd wake up in the middle of the night in, like, a sweat."

Linda scowled. "Did he say anything?"

"No"—Paula shook her head—"he'd just say it was nightmares."

Linda nodded and stirred her iced tea with the straw.

"Anyway," Paula continued, "everything just stopped after a while. The kids came, and everything. He never said anything about it." She shrugged. "I just didn't want to push it." She looked up. "Maybe that was a mistake on my part. I don't know."

Linda stirred her iced tea pensively, then looked up and smiled. "Hey!" she said. "Everything is going to be okay, huh? It'll be fine."

The reassurance was forced, Paula knew. She was suddenly embarrassed for having revealed her problem to Linda. "I'm sorry."

"It's okay," Linda said. Her optimism was hollow. "These are just tough times, but you'll see it through.

I know you will. Part of the problem is that it seems as though it will never end, but the wheel of fortune keeps on spinning, and the great pendulum will swing back."

"You're right," Paula said, trying to find refuge in some notion of destiny. She smiled. "Thanks."

For weeks Luke and Tim had been inseparable during the day. They each had interviewed for about thirty-five jobs with no luck, and they had encouraged each other and guided each other through the frustration. Tim had talked about Luke so much that he finally decided to invite him home for dinner so Paula and the kids could meet him.

They never entertained. Tim didn't believe in drawing strangers into the warm context of his family life. He was very guarded and protective about his family and home. And so he seemed a bit nervous and excited that Luke was coming, and he checked and rechecked with Paula to make sure the roast beef would be top quality and the house would be clean and the children well behaved. Perhaps Timothy wanted to display his home life as near perfect to show Luke how it would be when he returned to his wife and son. Perhaps he put an inordinate value on Luke's opinion, and he wanted that opinion to be favorable. Perhaps he wanted to merge this new friendship with the love and trust and hope he enjoyed in his family. Perhaps all of these together were motives, and the many dimensions to his invitation and Luke's acceptance certainly made the event exciting.

When they pulled into the driveway in Luke's old car, Ronnie was sitting on the front steps playing with his toy dump trucks and graders. He had been told to be on his best behavior, and so when Tim announced proudly to Luke, "There's my boy!" and called, "Ronnie, come here. I want you to meet somebody," the boy's eyes opened suspiciously, and he turned and ran around to the back of the house.

Tim seemed upset. "Hey, Ronnie!" he called, fatherly authority in his voice.

Luke touched Timothy's arm. "Let him be, man. He's just scared. You know, a stranger and all." Luke smiled. "Let him be."

"Yeah, sure." Timothy nodded. "Kids." He realized this initial encounter would not spoil the entire evening. "Come on, dinner must be almost ready." As Tim turned to enter the house, Luke again touched his arm and urged him to turn around face-to-face. When Tim looked questioningly into his eyes, Luke seemed embarrassed. "Uh, thanks," was all he said, but Tim knew then, instinctively, how much the evening would mean to Luke.

"You haven't tasted the food yet, man," Tim said lightheartedly, and he jabbed Luke in the arm. "Come meet my gorgeous wife! But keep your hands to yourself!"

Although she was busy in the kitchen, Paula stopped everything when they entered the house, and she wiped her hands on her apron and held them out to Luke. It showed in Luke's face how surprised he was at Paula's beauty and warmth.

"I'm so glad you could come tonight," she said.

"So am I," Luke said, looking around at the house. He inhaled the fragrant aroma of the cooking food. "Bachelor life isn't exactly conducive to home cooking." And he smiled, looking around. Ellen was peeking shyly around a corner. "Who's that?" he asked playfully, and she vanished.

"Have a beer?" Tim asked.

"Sure." Tim took two beers from the refrigerator

and handed one to Luke. They popped them open in celebration.

"I think I'll join you!" Paula said. She rarely drank, and it pleased Tim that she considered the occasion special.

At first Tim was nervous and anxious that everything would go all right. He did not want Luke to be depressed by the warmth and cohesion of his home and to compare it to what he had lost. He wanted Luke to see and to enjoy and perhaps even become a part of his home, and he wanted to help Luke however he might to get back with his own wife and son.

But Luke was wonderful. Truly a loving father, he charmed both Ellen and Ronnie and romped through the living room with them. They soon lost their fear of a stranger, a bearded stranger in their midst, and they brought out their favorite toys to display for him. Believing he would need to act as host, Timothy was pleasantly surprised when he could sit back and watch Luke and the children play.

Dinner exceeded all their expectations. The roast beef was done perfectly, and the garnishes and vegetables had turned out deliciously. Luke kept commenting on how good everything was. "Oh, we eat this way every night," Tim joked, and together the two children scolded, "Dad!" for the obvious fib.

For his part Luke did not seem troubled by the warmth of Tim's home. Instead he enjoyed their company; it seemed to him now more likely that he might solve the problems with his own wife. Enviously he watched how Paula served the dinner, how she coaxed the children to finish their meals, how she doted on Tim, but his envy was not selfish or sad, it was admiring and joyful.

"Whew!" he said when he had finished his dinner.

What a feast!" He folded his napkin. "Where's that diner you work at again?" he asked.

"I don't cook!" Paula protested. "I only wait on customers."

"I'd weigh three hundred pounds if I lived here," Luke said, and he playfully filled his cheeks with air and made a funny face at the children.

"Hope you have room for dessert," Tim said.

"Dessert? No way!"

"Strawberry shortcake," Ronnie said.

"Well, in *that* case!" Luke said. "I guess I'd better find room." He started to clear the table.

"Hold it," Tim said. "We have a professional waitress in our midst."

"All the more reason she should have the night off," Luke said. "You don't know what a pleasure I would consider it to do the dishes."

"Let him! Let him!" Ellen pleaded. It was usually her job to scour the pans.

"You don't get the chance to do dishes when all you eat are TV dinners." Luke laughed, and he stood and began clearing the table.

After dessert they sat together in the living room. Tim and Paula sat on the sofa and Luke sat in the easy chair. Tim lay his head in Paula's lap and watched. Charmed by this new person, Ronnie and Ellen curled up with him in the chair. They had changed into their pajamas and Luke playfully enacted some Three Stooges routines and held them and told them stories and riddles.

"Hey, Ronnie," he asked, "do you snore at night?"

"No."

"How do you know if you're asleep? How can you tell?"

"My ears are open," Ronnie responded, but he didn't

seem satisfied with the answer to a question he had never posed himself before.

"Ah," Luke said, raising his eyebrow and rolling his eyes, "but *how* do you know?"

"Because my ears are open!" Ronnie protested. He pointed to his ear.

"Okay," Luke said, "I'll buy that. I'm going to give you another piece of gum." He unpeeled the wrapper. "If you pop your muscles and show them to me one time, I'll give you this delicious piece of bubble gum."

Ronnie pulled his shirt, flexed his arm, and smiled proudly. Luke kneaded the muscle, then rolled his eyes at Ellen.

"Oh, boy, are we in trouble!" He turned to Ronnie. "But you won," he admitted. "I'll give you the gum. Here's one for you," he said, fumbling with the wrapper, "and one for you," he said, giving a piece to Ellen.

"He really must miss his kid," Tim whispered to Paula.

"Are you in the scouts yet?" Luke asked Ronnie.

"No," Ellen chimed in, very much the older sister. "He's too young."

Luke hugged her tightly. "What are you, the Big Girl? Huh?"

Ellen was suddenly embarrassed and hid her face as Luke rubbed his face against hers.

"Are you trying to hide from me? I'll rub my whiskers on you!" he said, deliberately rubbing his salt-and-pepper beard against her smooth cheek. She squealed and waved her hands in the air. "Stop! Stop!"

"What are you looking at?" Luke said to Ronnie. He grabbed them both and tickled them.

"Let's get him!" Ronnie cried, and he and Ellen double-teamed him.

"Hey, hey!" Paula called from the couch. "Leave Luke alone. It's time to get to bed."

"You've done it now." Tim nodded. "They'll never leave you alone."

Paula stood and held out her hand. "Come on, come on."

"Can Luke tuck us in?" Ellen pleaded.

"No," Paula said. "Luke can't tuck you in."

"Why not?" Ellen said, looking from her mother to her new friend.

"I don't mind," Luke said. "I don't mind."

"Are you sure?" Paula asked, outwardly pretending it would be an imposition but inwardly wondering how far she could trust this stranger.

"Please, Mom!" Ellen and Ronnie said.

Paula yielded to their instincts. "Okay," she said, waving her hand toward the bedroom. "They're yours."

Luke stood up and guided the children toward the bedroom.

"He was awfully good with the kids," Paula said when she and Tim lay together in bed that night.

"He's a great guy," Tim said.

"It's truly sad that he isn't with his own son. What happened with his wife, do you know?"

"He doesn't talk about her very much," Tim said, staring up into the darkness. "But I have the impression it's your usual GI blues story, the 'Nam story revisited." He rolled over onto his stomach. "Many wives can't handle the depression and the moods. Instead of helping their husbands through it, they take the easy way out." He looked at Paula and smiled. "We're so very lucky. I love you, Paula, and it means so very much to me that you try to understand." He stroked her hair.

"We are so very lucky," she agreed, and she pressed

her cheek into his back. "To have all this, a home, two beautiful children, and each other, what else could we ask for?"

"A job," Tim said. "It'll come. It'll come soon."

Paula stroked his back and her finger traced along the shrapnel scar below his right shoulder blade. She bent and kissed the scar in the same way a mother kisses a child's scrape to make it better.

"It looks like it's going to disappear someday," she whispered.

"No," Tim said quietly, "it'll always be there."

Paula caressed his shoulders and kissed the nape of his neck. "I love you," she whispered.

"I love you," he answered.

Chapter 7

When the mortar exploded, his head cleared, and he had a sense of timelessness and spacelessness, a clear vision of himself and his situation. He was flying through the air, and the ground was rushing up at him. He tucked his head as he had learned to do long ago in gym class, and the ground came up at him and he was rolling, and dirt and leaves were flying all about him.

He heard the rotors of the Huey beating the wind. Safety. Escape. He must make it to the Huey! Another shell rocked the ground, and he tried to raise his arm. He feared he was paralyzed, but his arm responded, then his leg. Nearby he heard Sanchez groaning, and he looked over to see the bone of his left arm sticking through the skin, a grisly white framed by shreds of muscle and gore.

"Please don't leave me," Sanchez pleaded.

"We'll make it, man!" he screamed to Sanchez. "Let's go, man!" And Tim, no longer thinking about himself leaped to his feet and helped Sanchez up. As long as he could get Sanchez to that copter. He would be all right if only he could get Sanchez there. Rescuing Sanchez was the most important thing he had ever done, he knew, and the little Puerto Rican, with the most beautiful face he had ever seen simply because it assured Tim he himself was still alive, grimaced in pain as he cried, "Help me, man. Help me." Up they pulled him. The gunner was spraying the jungle with lead to keep the sniper fire low, and the pilot hauled Sanchez into the Huey. Tim clambered in behind.

"Rafer, man?" Sanchez cried.

"He's dead," Tim said.

"Oh, my fucking God!" Sanchez said. "Oh, no, man, not Rafer!"

And Tim swallowed hard and he wanted to cry, the shock, the panic, and the raw fear now overwhelming him in waves of nausea until he saw the Badman.

On his knees, blood pouring from open wounds, his arms outstretched, pleading, his mouth wide open as if in prayer, pleading for Tim, the Badman screaming for Tim to help, "Don't leave me, man! Don't leave me! Please don't leave me!" And the trees of the jungle lashing to the wind whipped by the Huey's rotor, and the crackling of fire along the muggy periphery of the jungle, and Badman on his knees, on his fucking knees pleading, "Please! Please! Please don't leave me!" And the blood staining his field jacket. "Badman!" Tim screamed. "Badman! I won't leave you! Badman! Badman! Bad—"

Tim bolted upright in bed, sweat streaming down his face. He tried to catch his breath and his heart felt as though it would burst through his rib cage. He ooked toward Paula. She was sleeping soundly in the orange glow of the clock-radio dial.

Slowly, stealthily he rose from the bed. He crept to he bureau and opened the bottom drawer, taking out a small box. He opened it and rummaged through his war medals and snapshots until he found the picture. He held it up. On the left was Rafer, in the center was Sanchez, and on the right was himself. The picture had been torn carefully, and there was no face or body connected to the arm and hand with fingers from a black glove that encircled Tim's neck. The Badman. On his knees, pleading arms outstretched, covered in blood. "Please! Please don't leave me! Please! Please!" A grown man crying, his mouth sobbing, "Please!" and the diesel stink of the Huey and the pilot and gunner screaming at each other, "Get the fuck out of here! We'll all die, goddamnit!" And Tim screaming, "Badman! Badman!"

He shook his head to clear it. "I've got to get rid of this shit," he murmured. "Now. Tonight. Forever." And he tiptoed out of the bedroom, through the kitchen to the back door and out to the side of the garage. He lifted the lid of the garbage can and tossed in the medals and photos, then pulled out his black headband and his knife.

He had called the headband "The Black Halo." He never removed it. He believed that as long as he wore the black headband he was invincible, he could not be killed. It was not a superstition, it was karma. He projected out from himself the confidence and swaggering courage that he would survive, that he was "badder" than any of them, that he could rise above all of the shootings and burnings and greasings and fraggings, all the booby traps and firefights and shellings, that he would walk through the Valley of Death, and that he would keep walking, protected by the black headband like some comic-book superhero, out the other end of the valley and back home.

Timothy Murphy, there in the dead of night, had a strong impulse to put the headband on once more before he threw it out. *Karma, man.* It had successfully protected him for twelve months, three weeks, four hours, and seventeen minutes—his tour of duty from plane to plane. He scanned the sleeping neighborhood. Ordinary, common, normal. The one-story houses did not reach far into the dark, whirling void of sky. "Charlie's coming," a voice whispered at his ear. "The word is out. Charlie's coming tonight." The voice was low, insidious, and unnerving. A dark breeze rattled the palm trees. Charlie was out there, and Charlie would stalk him, and Charlie would surprise him. He squinted. He tried to see above, beyond, beneath, behind the false Hollywood stage of suburban America. Charlie lurked there. Charlie had nailed together this tacky little ghost town to trick him. Charlie wanted him, and Charlie was coming to get him tonight.

Naked except for black track shorts, Timothy Murphy squatted down and searched to his left and to his right. Instinctively he placed the headband around his forehead and reached to the ground, picked up mud, and smeared it on his forehead, cheeks, nose, and chin to dull the reflection of light. He knew Charlie was at the wire. He could hear him breathing. He could hear Charlie's heart beating. They'd taken away his weapon, but at least he had his knife. He inspected the long steel blade and felt with satisfaction the razor-sharp edge. He gritted his teeth, thinking of the pleasure he would have sinking the blade to the hilt into Charlie's vitals, again, again, again.

No, motherfucker, Charlie wasn't going to get him.

The loud screech of a guitar solo played in his ear, "It's a rock'n'roll show, motherfucker," the white lightning scream of guitar, the pounding bass drum, and Charlie out there waiting, waiting. Rock and fucking roll. Timothy Murphy grinned. No, no, no, the motherfucker wasn't going to get him. He heard something to his left. Like a panther, suspicious, wary, the fear clearing his head of every stray thought and fragment. Charlie and him, and he would walk away, motherfucker.

The guitar lick grew impossibly loud, and the bass drum pounded in his temples. Timothy Murphy sneered. He felt a tingling in his testicles and warmth in his vitals. Tonight you're going to die, Charlie, so pray to your Buddha, motherfucker.

Ronnie had heard the lid of the garbage can rattle, and he was thirsty. After visiting the bathroom, he padded out to the kitchen to get a glass of water. First he put his stool near the cabinets, then he climbed up and took a glass from the shelf. He put the glass upon the counter, then moved the stool to the sink. Carefully he poured water into the glass. He heard the screen door open, and he was scared. He looked around the corner to see who was coming into his house so late at night, and to his surprise and shock he saw his father on all fours prowling with wide suspicious eyes, a long combat knife in his teeth. He almost cried out. He almost spilled the water. He could tell this was no game. He backed away and listened.

Why was his dad doing this? Would he hurt him? Ronnie looked at the clock above the kitchen range. He watched the second hand go around and around and around. He listened for some noise, some sign of movement, but he heard nothing.

Ronnie backed against the kitchen cabinet and tried

to make himself flat. If Daddy didn't see him, maybe he could go back to bed. He listened, terrified. His voice caught in his throat and he could not speak. His hand shook and he feared he would spill the water. He pulled the water back and held it against his stomach.

Still the keen, white-hot metallic guitar lick screamed, and the bass drum pounded out the beat. "Charlie! You're there, you slant-eyed motherfucker, I know you're there, and I'm going to find you and decorate my watch chain with your balls." Through the jungle Timothy Murphy crept, stalking the source of his fear. "When I kill you, it will be gone, it will be all gone and I can go home. If I just bury you, I can go home, so now it's time to come out and fight because I'm going to grease you." He heard a noise behind a fallen tree (the counter) and he grinned, baring his teeth. It was Charlie! He'd given himself away. Around the roots of an aged banyan tree (the dining-room table and chairs) he crept, taking the knife from his teeth. He'd spring knife-first upon Charlie and slit his fucking throat before he could suck in another breath. He was behind that fallen log; though Timothy Murphy couldn't see him, he could sense him in the heavy dark night. He held his knife out and crept ever so slowly, ever so deliberately to the edge of the fallen log.

With his head against the kitchen cabinet, speechless and breathless with fear, Ronnie could feel his bowels loosen. He looked out the side of his eye, holding back his breath, his scream, his bowels, holding all within, when suddenly he saw the knife.

Around the corner it came, silver in the darkness, and he knew now he would die. He saw his father's other hand on the floor and was waiting, waiting and praying and holding everything in, sick at heart, when a dog barked.

Ready to pounce upon Charlie and slash him into oblivion with the knife, Timothy Murphy heard at his back a dog barking. Charlie was elsewhere, in the other direction. Slowly, stealthily, he turned and started toward the pathway (outdoors) to find Charlie where he lurked.

Again Ronnie heard the screen door open, and he dashed down the hall, sloshing water out of the glass, to lock himself in the bathroom.

Timothy Murphy awoke the next morning with a profound headache to the sound of the garbage truck. He hadn't been drinking heavily with Luke the night before, but he felt as though he had a terrible hangover. He looked at the clock. It was eleven-thirty. The kids had gone to school and Paula had gone to work and he had overslept. What the hell was going on here, anyway?

Then a dim memory of placing his medals into the garbage can came to him. For a moment he regretted throwing them out, but then he remembered dreaming the dream about Badman, the dream that would never go away, never as long as he lived. He had been awarded a medal for saving Sanchez. The medal was always a reminder of Badman. It was better that he had disposed of the medals and the photos. It was about time. With satisfaction he listened to the garbage truck progress up the street. Tim arose and saw to his amazement "The Black Halo" on his dresser. Why hadn't he thrown that out, too? He opened the bottom drawer and threw it in among his work clothes and sweat shirts. Time to shower and get back out to the streets and find a job.

Chapter 8

So she decided to do it, something she had wanted to do for a long time. The tension within—"how support-ive should I be, how much can I stand"—finally reached a critical point and began to eat away at her. Oh, she wished it didn't have to come to this, she wished it would all solve itself and be gone, and he could take Ronnie to Little League and all would be all right. But she knew something needed attention, and so she took the practical approach: she sought advice.

When thinking about where to turn, she had at first turned to Carmen at work. Carmen had a devil-may-care attitude toward fate that Paula admired. Yet Carmen wanted to take her side in a contest that hadn't materialized. Carmen wanted to posit a Paula-versus-Timothy situation while Paula wanted to posit her *and* Timothy versus the world. So Paula turned elsewhere for help. Tim had come back from Luke's apartment with a folder in his pocket—the vet center. Paula retrieved that folder, as if it represented the key to a riddle, and she called and made an appointment. And she still was not sure she had done the right thing. She wanted someone to tell her she had done the right thing and nobody would. Was she "snitching" on him? Was she overreacting? Was she being a busybody and just aggravating whatever problem might be there? Was she prying into Timothy's private life, a life he held apart, chose to hold apart, and wanted to continue to hold apart from her? And yet she believed she herself needed to talk to someone and so that justified it sufficiently.

Rob, who ran the vet center, tried to help. He listened and asked tough questions, then listened some more. Rob himself had a deep reservoir of grief and pain that he dammed up and would not release. Sorrow showed in the lines of his face. He himself was a Viet Nam war veteran.

"Has it grown intolerable?"

"Look," she said, "I don't even know if I'm in the right place, so ..." What she left unspoken meant more than it would have if she had said it straight out.

"Oh," Rob said, "maybe it isn't, then maybe it is. Let's talk about it anyway. What made you think about coming here?"

"Well, I uh, I found this in my husband's coat. I believe it's a sign that he's searching, too." She winced. She hated to be under pressure. She handed him the pamphlet that Tim had lifted from Luke's apartment, the pamphlet about the vet center.

"Can you be a little bit more specific about your husband?" Rob asked. "Do you think he's going through changes now that are related to 'Nam?"

"Well," she snapped back impatiently, sarcastically, "I wouldn't be here if I didn't think that, would I?" The image of Tim, a can of beer in his hand, staring at the television as the national anthem signaled the end of another broadcasting day, as jet fighters soared through the wild blue yonder, Tim sneering and putting the beer to his lips and nodding—that image haunted her. It had been like that once before. He would sit, staring into the blank television screen, his hand on his .357 Magnum. She never knew what he was thinking of doing with the gun, whether he wanted to shoot out the television screen or shoot himself. It terrified her. She pleaded with him to get rid of the gun because the children were getting older, and finally he had done so. No threat of a midnight prowler could engender fear as intense as the fear she felt seeing her husband like that.

"I told you I found that in his pocket. And . . . the other morning when I was taking out the garbage, I found his medals. He was throwing them away."

"That's not unusual," Rob said. "A lot of the vets will try to throw away anything that reminds them of 'Nam. It's much harder, though, if not impossible to get rid of the memories." Rob smiled sympathetically. "What is his name?"

Paula bristled up. "I'm not going to tell you his name!" she said defensively. "I don't want you to call him up and tell him I came here."

Rob grimaced and nodded. These first encounters were always the most delicate. "Do you think he'd be willing to come down to a meeting?"

"No," Paula said emphatically. The hopelessness of her own situation was being revealed profoundly to her. She was asking for help, and as it was offered, she had to refuse it. Was it pride? Was it fear? She felt a sob welling up within at the despair.

"Would *you* be willing to come to a meeting of the wives?" Rob asked. Tears flowed down her face as Paula struggled unsuccessfully to control the flood of emotions. "It'll help you to understand your husband a lot better if you can sit down and communicate with women that have had a very, very similar experience."

Had other women suffered through this? she asked herself. Often it felt as though she were so alone, the only person who had ever suffered through this problem. Could it be worse for some of them? How did they cope? "Yeah," Rob said comfortingly.

"If it'll help my husband," Paula sobbed from both apprehension and relief, "I'll do anything, *anything*." At least there was something further to be done.

Rob nodded his head and smiled, and they discussed when the next meeting would be. Paula searched in her mind for pretexts she might use about where she was going, at least during the first few meetings. As she stood to leave, she dried her tears, reached out her hand, and took Rob's. "Thank you," she said, "thank you so very much!"

"We're here to help you," he said. "We'll do everything we can to help you."

Paula walked from the office with her head buzzing. It was a tremendous relief to know others were around to help her, yet it was such a huge step to reach out and admit that the problem had grown larger than her ability to handle it. Friday was the next morning. She looked forward to hearing what the other women had suffered through, and she would choose the stories she told with great care. The sun was out as she made her way along the street, and she heard the happy sounds of children on bicycles and roller skates. Perhaps everything would be all right. That was all she asked.

Chapter 9

Another day of job hunting. Applications to fill out, snobby clerks looking down their noses, interviews to be scheduled. Timothy Murphy hated it, and he thought it would never end. By afternoon they were again out near the airport and Tim had an appointment scheduled with the foreman of a shipping firm.

"This will be your lucky break," Luke said as he approached the building. "I can feel it, man." He clenched his fist and gritted his teeth and leaned his head back. "A nice, fat, easy, high-paying job!" he cried.

"It's only a loader's position," Tim said. "They're not looking for a chief executive officer."

"You'll wow them. You'll be president of the board inside of two years."

"Let's just hope they take me on as a loader," Tim said, joshingly punching Luke's arm.

"Good luck, man," Luke said. He sat down on step to a loading dock. "I'll wait out here."

Timothy Murphy waited twenty minutes to be shown by a middle-aged woman into the cramped messy office of Hugh Baxter, loading-dock foreman. Baxter had the swollen florid complexion of a beer drinker with many years invested in a particular brand, and he smoked a cigar each afternoon to hide the smell on his breath of his two lunchtime "pops."

"Si'down," he said, scanning Tim's application. He looked up. "You can handle a fast pace when we gotta move a truck an hour?"

"I've seen worse," Tim said. "Sure."

"You understand there's no union, and no chance a union will somehow spring up."

"I want a job," Tim said candidly. "I don't want to make anyone's life tougher than necessary."

Baxter nodded. "Good. Do you understand you'll be working directly for me, answerable to me for everything, and that I demand punctuality and respect?"

Timothy Murphy smiled. "I'm your man!"

The foreman sat back, puffing on his cigar. "Looks good," he said, pointing to the application. "I think we can use you."

Tim breathed a sigh of relief and he smiled widely. "Man, it's good to hear those words again."

The foreman leaned back and drew in a long puff of cigar smoke. "Yeah," Baxter said, "I bet things have been hard out there."

Timothy Murphy smiled broadly for the understanding of his plight. "You ain't kidding," he said.

"Yeah." Baxter nodded. "How about ... can you start next Monday?"

"Man," Tim said, beaming radiantly, "I can start today. I've got no more problems at all." Tim couldn't wait to tell Luke. This job was a good omen, and it wouldn't be long until Luke landed one, too.

"Fine, fine," the man said. "How about a cup of coffee?" He rose and poured himself a cup.

"Uh, no. No thanks," Tim said, waiting to take his first order from Baxter.

Baxter sat back down. "You know, I noticed on your application you were in Viet Nam."

"Yes, sir, I was there." Tim became almost rigid, as if talking with a commanding officer.

"I was in the corps myself." Heavily he sat in the chair and it creaked as he leaned back. "Yeah," he considered, "now that was a *real* war."

Tim sensed the recrimination about to come, and he braced himself. A *real* war. All wars are real wars. What an idiot! He nodded in agreement because he needed the job. "Yes, sir, I'm sure it was."

Baxter leaned over the desk to drive home a point. "I landed on Iwo Jima, second wave in. You know, I went to basic training with a kid named Alie Kyle. Good old Alie. He was the first one to get it." He motioned as if his hand held a pistol. "Soon as the doors opened on that landing craft."

Tim felt sweat breaking on his forehead, and he wondered how long and how often this talk would go on. He tried to avoid the foreman's eyes. Yeah, a real war. His stomach churned as he looked again into the well. Four or five bodies of GIs lying facedown in that well, their hands tied behind their backs, and the furry rats scurrying over their raw flesh, and the worms sliding in and out of their skin.

"We had it bad back then, kid. I mean real, fucking bad. It was a *war*!"

"What is this asshole's purpose?" Timothy Murphy asked himself, and involuntarily a scene came back.

In the Huey, he was sitting toward the back near pile of boots. Just boots, used combat boots. The Huey dipped and a boot tipped over, and slowly blood spilled out of it. "Hey," Tim had cried to the pilot, his face ashen, "take it easy as you go!"

Baxter stood and walked around the desk, holding his coffee cup. He wanted to prove something to Tim and Tim shrank into the chair, wishing he could vanish.

"I mean, we fought for close to three weeks until we even looked like we were getting any control of that little fucking island." He nodded. "But we did. We finally dislodged the fucking Jap."

The Jap, Tim thought, Charlie, the gook, the slope, the slant-eyed motherfucker—what difference did it make? Who cared? Just forget it, forget you ever fought and killed, forget it, goddamnit! And still Baxter prattled on!

It was the eyes that gave combat duty away, you could always tell by the eyes. The shape and the face could be of a nineteen-year-old kid, but the eyes were aged, weary with experience of the world. Sunken and dark around the edges, twitching and suspicious, it was a look, a sardonic, ironic stare that fixed you, sized you up, catalogued where to hit, where to shoot, where to slide in the shiv when the shit hit the fan, a weary, tired, embittered look. No drug, no rock solo, no piece of ass, no roller coaster ride aboard a Huey could shock you like that look.

Timothy Murphy was leaning on a cane, R&R after the firefight that took Rafer and Badman. A slim, freckled towhead of a kid from Nebraska elbowed up to him at the bar. "Beer," the kid said to the Hawaiian bartender.

"I'll need to see some proof that you're of age," the bartender said. And the kid looked at Tim, and the look in his eye showed he had lived through the apocalypse. The kid nodded at Tim, staring deeply into his soul, and Tim did the same. Then the kid looked back at the bartender.

"I want a beer, and I want it now," he said.

"I'm terribly sorry, sir. I'd be glad to get you any brand you might like if I can just see some proof of age."

A waitress was passing by from the waitress station with a tray of four beers. The kid pulled two bottles off the tray and stuffed a twenty-dollar bill into her bodice. Then all hell broke loose with white mice and MPs and the entire world rushing in to collar an eighteen-year-old kid. Tim left by the back door. Tim now remembered and wanted to leave by the back door, but Baxter hovered above him.

"You know what the tragedy is about Viet Nam?" he asked.

No, asshole, Tim screamed silently to himself, his jaw set and his teeth grinding. *I had to come to you to find out. Tell me what the tragedy is!*

The man threw out his arms expansively. "Nobody really knew why the hell we were there. I mean in WW2 we made the world safe for democracy. But you—" He shook his head. "You guys were just jerking yourselves off."

"Yes, well I guess . . ." Tim started to say.

Not paying attention to him, Baxter continued. "You know, I've got a kid just about your age. You know how he got out of that war?" He pointed to his temple. "Smart kid, smart." He licked his lips and nodded. "Went out and found a doctor, had him write a letter to say he had a bad back." Baxter winked. "That's how he got out."

Tim held his head in his hands, nearly retching with nausea.

"First, of course, I was *really* pissed," Baxter continued. Draft dodging, Europe, Canada, on the lam from the army, the fatherland, self-respect, better to live to fight another day. "I mean," the man said, "when you get called to serve your country, you go." He shrugged. "Just like I did."

And sick at heart, the images of a poem he'd read long ago played through Timothy Murphy's ear—think, think of anything . . .

. . . Gas canisters, the green underwater murk of a gassed trench in World War I, the gagging soldiers, lungs boiling with blood, the body cart, then: "It is sweet and noble to die for your country."

And still Baxter kept on!

"Sorry to have to say it, but"—he returned to his seat behind the desk—"the old U.S. government, Johnson, Nixon, you know, they really had you pulling." He made a masturbatory gesture. "They really sucked you in. Nobody honestly wanted to go to Viet Nam!" He threw out his arms and said in astonishment, "There was nothing there. Nothing but a sucker's war. That's all it was," he taunted his new employee, "a sucker's war."

Seething with rage for the fat, mottled face, Timothy Murphy stood and clenched and unclenched his fists, then he sprang at the desk and shoved the entire heap of clutter to the floor. "You bastard!" he screamed. "You're like them all! You don't understand!" And now, worked into a fury, he seized a chair, raised it high above his head, and slammed it down onto the desk. It split and Timothy Murphy hammered the back and the seat of the chair against the desk, again,

again. Hugh Baxter, afraid of a beating, cowered back against the wall.

Outside, Luke heard the screaming and the banging, and he dashed through the outside office where secretaries and laborers were milling about, wondering if they should enter the combat.

"You son of a bitch!" Tim screamed, and Luke saw which door the screams came from, and he dashed to it, ripped it open, and grabbed Tim, who by then was standing above Hugh Baxter, physically threatening him with a leg of the chair.

"Tim!" Luke cried. "Tim! What's going on here?" Luke looked from one to the other of them, then he seemed to read what had taken place. "What did you do?" he whispered hoarsely at Baxter.

The foreman stood up in shock, nearly swallowing his cigar as Luke tried to pull Tim back.

"Come on, man!" he shouted. "Let's get out of here!"

"Don't you *ever*, man, don't you ever say that again." Menacingly, Tim waved the stick from the chair in Baxter's nose. Baxter was sputtering about the police and a lawsuit and other such things as Luke wrestled Tim toward the door. "Come on, man, you don't need this."

"You remember what I said," Tim cried threateningly. "You son of a bitch!"

"Okay," Luke said to Tim, "game time. You want to take it out? You want to take this place out?"

Suddenly Tim saw what he had done. "No," he said. "No. Come on, man."

"You." Luke pointed at Baxter. "You're lucky! You're one lucky son of a bitch!"

Then Luke hauled Tim through the door, and they confronted the faces of employees. Both broke into a run; they fled through the door and sprinted across the parking lot.

"Pisses me off," Tim said later, after he explained what had happened in the office. They were sitting in the Statue of Liberty Bar again. "The same rap from everyone, everywhere. Man, our lily-white asses were on the line out there in the bush, while they were sitting safe, secure, and warm over here, and they blame us for the fuck-ups of politicians. What the hell did we know?"

Luke stretched out his arm. "Just the way of the world, partner."

"Yeah," Tim said. "Sure." He realized he was lapsing into self-pity, so he searched elsewhere for his criticism. "The irony of the fucking event was that I could have greased him just like that." He snapped his finger. "I'm out looking for work, anything that'll come along, and the one thing I can do well, killing, isn't a marketable skill. Pisses me right off!"

"Have another beer," Luke coaxed him. "It'll mellow you out."

"Sure," he said sardonically, and he held up two fingers.

When Ellen came running to her screaming, "Mommy, Mommy, Ronnie is killing my baby!" Paula dashed into the bedroom where indeed Ronnie was attempting to plunge a rubber knife into the plastic skin of a doll.

"Just what are you doing, young man?" she asked, whereupon he whipped around and hid the knife behind his back.

"Nothing!" he said quickly.

"What are you doing to Ellen's doll?"

Ronnie closed his mouth and offered his tightened lip up to her defiantly. "He said he'd kill my baby," Ellen whined. "He said so. He did." And she pointed her finger accusingly. With more anger than she usually used to chastise the children, Paula took the knife away from Ronnie; then, when he refused to tell her where he learned such a trick, she spanked him. He cried freely, wailing at the pain of the spanking, the disgrace of being caught, and at something else, at the fear he still felt from seeing his father prowling through the living room with a knife.

"Now," Paula said with discipline in her voice, "you stand in the corner until you can tell me where you learned to do such bad things."

And sobbing, miserable, humiliated, and all alone, Ronnie turned to the wall, away from her and from his sister, to face his punishment. For an hour and a half he stood facing the wall. He thought about many things, about school, about his playmates, about the dog that scared him up the street, about the fair, about the circus his dad took him to last year, about some of the things some of the guys said in the school yard about his dad, and he stood there stoically, vowing never to give up his secret.

Paula's new approach, though, changed his mind.

"Ronnie," she said sweetly, "you don't have to stand in the corner anymore."

He turned and looked up at her, hoping she would forgive him, but not quite sure whether he would forgive her.

"Come to Mama," she said, and she held out her arms. He tried to ignore this plea, but he was so scared and so bewildered that he bowed his head and ran to her, hugging her fiercely. "Oh, Ronnie," she cooed, "I love you." And he hugged her and burrowed his face into her neck. She stroked his back for a very long time, then she pulled him away from her and met his eyes with her own. "Mama loves you, Ronnie. And I don't like it when you treat Ellen's baby that way. Why did you do that to Ellen's baby?"

Ronnie's face dissolved, and he looked as though he would cry.

"Where did you learn to do such things?" Paula urged him gently.

Ronnie's lower lip extended in a truly classic pout. "I don't know," he lied.

"Tell me," Paula said, her suspicion mounting with his refusal to answer. "Please, son, tell me. Was it the boys at school?" He shook his head no. "Was it the television?" Again he shook his head no. "Was it anyone you know?" He nodded his head, then bit his lip, still afraid. "Who was it?"

"It was Daddy," he said shamefully. He hid his head against her breast again. He felt he had betrayed his father.

"When did Daddy show you that?" she asked.

"He didn't," Ronnie said. "I saw him. I saw him with a knife. He was coming to get me!" Again he snuggled his face into her breast, and he began to cry. Paula comforted him, then asked him to explain.

"I got up to get a glass of water, and I saw him. He had a knife, and his eyes were weird, and he had dirt on his face and a black ribbon around head."

"What was he doing?" she asked.

"He was crawling around the living room and the dining room with the knife, and he was looking for me."

"No, he wasn't, Ronnie. Daddy was just playing,"

she said lightly. "He was just playing a game that you didn't understand. He would never hurt you."

"No," Ronnie said. "He was trying to kill me."

And Paula tried to convince the boy otherwise as she rocked and comforted him, as she felt terrible about having punished him for so long, and as she looked with fear and trepidation into the future. Oh, no, she thought, oh, no, no, no. And her mind and heart grew sick at having to face the crisis she feared more than death itself—having to tell the man she loved that she might not be able to live with him anymore.

So near and yet so far away—Tim felt his anger seething. He had finally scored a job! The solution to all his problems had been within reach, only to be pulled away by the Great Joker. The Great Joker. Tim told Luke his theory of the Great Joker. The Great Joker was a malevolent force that watched while humans worked and toiled and hoped and prayed for things to go their way, and then just at the proper moment to make things truly interesting, the Great Joker would pull away what he could, cheating the poor deluded person of what he expected and hoped for. The Great Joker and Charlie were blood brothers, and they both had been working overtime lately.

Timothy Murphy did not have the courage or the desire to face Paula. Telling her of how he had exploded would shame him terribly, would reduce his self-esteem, and the scorn in her eye would be too much to bear. So he did the least smartest thing—he drank. No more job interviews, no more want ads, no more phone calls, he would use his last quarter to buy beers and drinks that would keep the pain away, that would make it leave forever.

Luke was by his side, his best buddy. Only Luke

could understand the terrible irony of Hugh Baxter's remarks and the luck of the foreman and the company that Tim had kept his rage focused on inanimate objects. Luke reassured him he had not overreacted, that he would have helped if Tim had wanted to "take the place out," to destroy everything and everyone there. The bartender was smoking a cigar, and Tim made three or four sarcastic references to it. Finally he snapped, "Will you put that fucking thing out?" The cigar reminded him of Hugh Baxter, and he was daring the bartender to react. They had been drinking all afternoon and the sour glow from the beer caused Tim to want a fight.

"No," the bartender said, pushing their money back at them, "but I'll put you out." He took their beers and dumped them in the sink, then gave them back two dollars each. "I don't need your patronage," he said with finality, "so hit the street."

Both men were utterly surprised. The bartender walked away from them toward the older men who drank beer and shots quietly all afternoon. Tim rolled his eyes at Luke and Luke winked. "Boy," Tim said, "we're striking out everywhere today."

"The Great Joker," Luke said, pocketing his money. "Come on."

Darkness was full and the wind was swollen with moisture. Tim picked up a stone in the road. "Fuck him!" he said. "Can't even drink in peace anymore." And he hurled the stone with great accuracy at the faded likeness of the Statue of Liberty above the bar. It hit with a hollow, empty sound, and Lady Liberty swung in the dark wind. They huddled down the street together.

Palm trees heaved on the wind as they made their way along the boulevard. More beer, more drinks, they wanted more to calm themselves, but they didn't want to drink indoors. Free at last, they wanted to enjoy the cool breeze of evening. They stopped at a liquor store and bought a six-pack and a bottle of rye. It was good to get drunk once in a while, Tim told Luke. It was good for the soul. It was necessary.

"I love this," Tim said, walking along the street sipping his beer in the open. "I love getting shit-faced." Defiantly he raised his beer bottle in the air. "Fuck yoooooooooou!" he screamed.

"Easy, man," Luke said. "You'll draw the heat, and frankly, after my investment in this load I can't afford bail."

Timothy Murphy now was swaggering in the middle of the deserted street. The street lamps cast an eerie orange glow on parked cars, on windows, and on the slick pavement. No one was walking. It seemed like an occupied city.

"We gotta get off the street," Luke said. "Hey, the ball field is nearby. Right over there. Let's go over."

"What?" Tim asked drunkenly.

"Let's go over to the football field and sit up in the stands."

"Man." Tim laughed, weaving and waving his beer bottle around. "You're nuts. A fucking football field! You jocks are all alike, once a jock always a jock." He looked at Luke askance. "I'll bet you fucking enlisted."

"What?" Luke asked, shocked.

"I'll bet you fucking enlisted, man. You dumb jock."

The pained expression on Luke's face told Tim, even in his drunken state, that he was right. "Uncle Sam grabbed me, man, but you *asked* to go over there?" He was puzzled. "Why?"

"It seemed like the right thing to do." Luke both wanted and didn't want to talk about it. They reached the fence to the football field and Tim handed him the six-pack.

"Here, you hold this while I jump over, then you hand it over to me." Tim tried to vault the fence, but he was too drunk and he couldn't make it. Luke walked along the fence to the gate, kicked it, and it squealed open. He walked to where Tim was still trying to vault the fence. He held the six-pack and knit his eyebrows with great interest at Tim's next attempt. "Degree of difficulty, eight-point-nine. Degree of sobriety, zero-point-zero. Will he make it, ladies and gentlemen?"

Tim grabbed the top bar of the fence. "I'll be damned. It was open," he said, and he vaulted over the fence and landed in a heap at Luke's feet.

"Good show!" Luke cried. "Good show!" And he handed Tim the six-pack.

Together they swayed out toward the field. "You know," Tim said, "I don't even know what that guy said to set me off, but it sure felt good."

"Didn't it feel good? I mean, I even felt good!" Luke spun upon the grass and swigged at a new beer. "Yahoo!" Suddenly he ran to the middle of the field where he spun and spun, trying to enhance his drunkenness with dizziness.

"Yahoo!" Tim joined him, and sat down with the six-pack.

"You see this, man?" Luke said, spreading his arms as if he were displaying something quite sacred.

"What?" Tim's brow knit, looking for what Luke was showing him.

Luke pulled off his jacket and threw it onto the ground. "This, man! This is the very sight of the greatest moment in my life. You only get one shot at a greatest moment in your entire fucking lifetime, and here is where I had mine. We were up twenty to sixteen with about a minute left to play in the game. Central. They were driving." Luke adopted the tone of a sportscaster, spreading his arms wide to suggest an imminent threat.

"They had the ball right on the twelve. Oh, man! I've got to show you this. It was pure mythology." Luke looked up for the crowd's reaction and the cheerleaders' screaming, but it was dark and blank and silent. He shook his head and grabbed Tim. "You're the guy from Central."

"No. I don't want to be."

"Yeah," Luke insisted. "You got to be the guy from Central. He's just a candy ass. His name is Webber. He's got this great grinning smile, the biggest hot dog you ever saw. Okay"—he positioned Tim—"all right. Now you stand there."

Tim squinted to find the line of scrimmage, but there was none. He just positioned himself opposite Luke.

"Okay," Luke called. "Hut, hut. I'm playing safety, and they send the guy out. That's you. Webber."

Tim staggered toward the goal line.

"Down and out, a pass pattern," Luke called, indicating the path with his index finger. "Okay. Now, I'm in the middle. I look over and you've just faked out our man that's covering you."

"Yeah." Tim staggered on. "I just faked you out, man."

"And so I haul ass after you. The quarterback releases the ball and there's Webber, *you*, man, Webber with his arms out. Put your arms out!" Luke ordered. "His arms out like a bushel basket waiting." Tim danced unmolested into the end zone. "Lift your arms and smile, you fuck!" Luke cried with great hilarity.

Tim raised his arms to the empty grandstands, and he danced about with great delight at being an open pass receiver in the end zone. Luke, then, bowed his head and ran full out at Tim, tackling him to the ground.

"And then I grab the ball as it pops free, and I've got that sucker, and I waltz a hundred and two yards for the final touchdown." Luke attempted to show his run. He raised his hands and smiled at the empty darkened grandstands. "And the crowd! They went nuts!"

Tim sat up, brushing himself off. "You made me spill my beer, you fuck."

"Fuck your beer," Luke said with rebuke. "I just told you the greatest moment of my life . . . and I lied about the touchdown!" Luke broke into joyful laughter as Tim looked up in disbelief. "Seventeen years," Luke said. "It's been seventeen years. That's how long ago it was. And I haven't had anything like it since."

Luke lay on the ground, tired, drunk, and depressed. Suddenly the stupidity of reliving that moment, so trivial and so long ago, washed over him, and he scowled. "Damn it! It wasn't supposed to be like this, you know?" Tim nodded. "It was supposed to be . . . different. It was supposed to be . . . better."

Drunkenly flicking a match, Tim managed to light a cigarette, then he cupped it and rolled over to Luke.

Luke continued his diatribe: "I didn't expect much. I didn't expect—I mean, no horseshit parade. Besides, when I got back from 'Nam, my fucking feet were killing me. Who wanted to march? I just expected to *live*. I just expected to live my life."

Luke sighed, and the sorrow of his voice echoed off the empty stands and the empty gridiron.

"I just wanted to have the love of my wife and my son, to be normal and ordinary," Luke said. Tim was silently nodding. "But somebody!" Luke said with anger. "Some *asshole* changed the rules of the game in the middle of the fucking play, and nobody dropped me a flag."

"The Great Joker, man," Tim said. Luke was worked up, as bitter as Tim had ever seen him, and he watched with great interest.

"I want to tell you, man," Luke said as if he were imparting some great secret, "sometimes I think that the guys we lost over there had it better off."

Tim closed his eyes. The Badman, he was better off. "Surviving," he said, agreeing, "coming back to this. That's the real hell."

"Come on, man," Luke said, raising his head, "I've had it with this football field. Let's find a bar."

They sauntered along the avenue looking for a quiet, cheap bar. They had time, since they still had part of the liquor and the six-pack to finish. At last they saw a place, Noah's Ark, and they paused. It was dark and dingy. Incredibly old alcoholics were hung from the bar railing. "Well," Tim said jauntily, "God told Noah one pair of every species, and I don't see any vets in there. Let's go."

Their moods had shifted. Now Tim was lighthearted and Luke was dour. It was as if Luke were suffering by proxy for what had happened at the trucking warehouse. He couldn't get his mind off the war.

"People back here don't understand it," he said. "Pisses me off. They pretend to be such great keepers of the peace and upholders of human rights, then they take out their frustration on vets. What happened to you this afternoon is so fucking characteristic!" He pounded the table. "Everybody needs somebody to blame, man. Pisses me off. We should have taken that place out!"

"It really got to you today, didn't it?"

"You bet your ass," Luke said, his eyes lurching around the bar.

"Easy, man. It's usually me they have to calm down."

"But how the fuck can they force you to confront such insane horror and not be affected? Sure, go defend your country, then come back whole and sane and heroic. Meanwhile the poor bastards missing a leg or a hand or their balls fill up the veterans' hospitals—they're warehoused away so that people don't need to be reminded. Bullshit, Tim. I'm sick of all the bullshit. Television fucked up the war. If we had some honcho like Patton, the war would have been over in a year. But they send us politicians and grafters who want to prolong it, don't know if they want to keep fighting, then can't explain why they were there in the first place. And we have to live with the bullshit the rest of our lives."

"You always have the consolation that you enlisted," Tim said to break the spell of his tirade.

Luke rolled his eyes.

"Something's eating away at you, friend." Tim sat back and smiled. "Tell me what it is."

Luke shook his head. "It's all fucked," he said, bitterly swigging at the beer bottle.

"Tell me," Tim urged.

Luke looked him full in the face for an entire minute. "You want to hear?" he asked.

"Sure." Tim shrugged.

"Well, I have a theory, man, that every mother's son who did time over there has one scene that crystallized the entire horror show, and that this scene keeps playing in their brain, and it'll never go away."

Tim nodded thoughtfully.

Luke took a long swallow of beer to ready himself for his account. "They came through the wire one night," he said. "I don't know how many. They came in waves, thousands, millions of them it seemed like. Like vermin they kept crawling in to get us, to dislodge us from our emplacement. We fired and fired. It was just a big wall of people coming at us. They overran our positions. I don't know what happened after that." He paused and looked up searchingly at Tim. "I still have dreams. They say we were overrun, that we fought hand to hand for over four hours. I don't know if it's true or not."

Tim reached across the table and clasped Luke's hand. He said nothing, though his mind, dulled by the beer, remembered his own private glimpse of hell. It was a dull ache. It was this precise dull ache, this numbness that came so often upon him. The Badman. Tim clasped Luke's hand still harder.

"The next day," Luke continued, "they found me alive. I was the only one there. I was still hugging this sapper. I was still hugging him . . . and . . . as I held him, I kept jabbing my knife into him. Life and death locked in a struggle until the bitter end."

Tim lifted up Luke's hand and squeezed it still tighter. He wanted to tell Luke his own scene. "Leave it there," he said to himself. "Don't take it home with you."

"Every now and then," Luke said, his sad eyes fixed on the spilled beer on the table, "I wake up in the middle of the night, and I see his face, that VC sapper. His eyes, they're open. And he's begging me. Please."

Luke broke down into sobs. His entire frame shook.

Sure, it was the beer and the bullshit of the afternoon,
Tim told himself, but it was that one look behind the
curtain, that one scarring look at fear and hell itself
that would never go away. He reached out and held
Luke as Luke hugged him. Luke sobbed against his
neck, and Tim held him as often he'd held his terrified
children in the dead of the night.

"It's all right, man. Come on," he whispered. "Let's
go home. Let's go home."

"Home," Luke repeated. Drunkenly they struggled
to their feet and left the bar.

She heard his drunken good-byes, and the car pulling away. She was furious.

As Tim entered the house, Paula was clearing the
table of the supper dishes. She did not look up. She
piled three sets of used dishes together, and she put
one unused set back in the cabinet. Deliberately, she
began washing the dishes. Routine and order were of
utmost importance—she tried to keep the house nice
for him, but now she didn't know. The revelation that
he had been prowling about the living room with a
knife suggested a crisis of tremendous proportion. If
she only washed the dishes and put them away, perhaps some part of it could be avoided.

"I'm home," she heard Tim say.

Her blood curdled. How dare he be drunk tonight?
she asked herself.

"Hey?" he repeated angrily, lumbering into the
kitchen, "I said I was home."

"If I just get these dishes done," Paula whispered to
herself, and she did not look up. "You're late," she
said, and she deliberately used a curt, unforgiving
voice to throw him off stride.

"I'm hungry," he said, and it sounded like a command. He tried to hug her.

"Then you should have come home when it was dinnertime," she said cuttingly.

"Come on, don't give me that shit!" Timothy Murphy said in a disgusted voice.

Paula went to the table and began to wipe it. Tim followed her and tried to grab her, but she pulled away in anger. "Stop it!"

Tim scowled.

If I can just get these dishes done and show him I can function in his absence, she thought to herself. She tried to ignore him.

"What the hell is wrong with you?" he said in derision.

"There's nothing wrong with me," she said right back to him. The tone of her voice unmistakably suggested there was something very wrong with him.

"Bullshit! Bullshit! Bullshit! Bullshit!" he cried. "What the hell is wrong with you?"

She turned on him and the showdown was one he should have known to avoid just by the look in her eye. "Just leave me alone. Just go off and fall asleep somewhere. Go take your drunken stupor somewhere else."

Tim seized her and spun her around. "Listen, lady," he growled. "I don't have to take this shit from you."

"Let go," she pleaded. "You're hurting me!"

"Well, then tell me what's wrong?"

Paula pulled free and glared at him. "Oh, there's nothing wrong." She stepped back and spoke sarcastically, "I mean, is this going to be the new thing now? You're going to start coming home drunk every night?"

Tim waved disgustedly and went to the refrigerator

to get a beer. "I don't need this shit," he said in disgust.

"Well," Paula screamed, "maybe I do!"

Tim tried to move past her, but she blocked his path. She wanted to force a confrontation on this issue and to have it resolved, but he didn't want to pursue anything. "Just forget it," he said.

"No," she said, spinning him about. "I'm not going to forget it." She looked into his eyes and the sight of his drunkenness disgusted her. "I want to know what the hell you think you were doing the other night."

"What night?" he asked haughtily.

"The night," Paula said with chilling anger, "that your son saw his father crawling around the house with a knife in his hand. *That* night." She sneered at him. "Damn it! What is wrong with you?"

Tim pulled open the refrigerator door and reached for a can of beer. Instead, he saw a plate of food, and so he pulled that out. "I don't know what the hell you're talking about," he said. He turned to walk away from her. The raw insistence in her voice nagged at him.

"You answer me," she pleaded. "You had your son scared half to death!" She followed him. No, she thought, it was all wrong, all wrong. All her efforts to put on a good front, a happy face, nothing she did was appreciated or reciprocated. Tim didn't care. Now, he wouldn't even face the consequences of his behavior, wouldn't even admit to some bizarre and unholy rite in the dead of the night. "What is wrong with you?" she cried.

"Just leave me alone," he said.

"We have to talk," Paula said insistently.

Talk, he thought, talk. Talk, talk, talk. Not talk but action. He looked down at her and saw for the first me the cowering human fear of her, the small, rembling, cowardly, and critical face, and he despised . He hated her suddenly. She didn't care about him. ucking dinner. He'd been late for dinner and now he was manufacturing some wild tale about him in he kitchen with a knife to play with his brain the xact same way that fucking Hugh Baxter had this fternoon. She didn't understand. A hundred vulgar words buzzed through his mind—twat, bitch, cunt, whore, slut—as he tried to cope with her anger and hysteria. He sneered at her. She was just like them all, teasing you along, playing fast and loose until hey sank their claws in, then they owned you. Then hey milked you and controlled you, and you couldn't even have a few beers with a buddy without them raising a hue and cry. He saw how angry, how afraid and crazed she was, and he attributed it all to showmanship. What a bitch!

She put her hands on her hips and stood her ground as if to mark her turf. "I want to know," she said, and he anger in her face infuriated him. What right did she have? How could she do this? Like that asshole Baxter this afternoon, where did she get off? He thrashed out to push her aside, and she resisted. She squealed at the force he applied to her, then she ripped away. Tim tried to push her again, but he missed his mark drunkenly and slapped her in the face. She fell against the counter, struggling to keep her balance. Then she fell headlong upon the kitchen floor.

Immediately Paula sat up. She glared at him with such hate that Tim backed away.

In his bed, Ronnie, who had been upset all day by the punishment, bolted up and listened. He knew something had just happened, because the noise had been

intruding upon his dreams and now there was ı
noise.

Tim saw blood appear on Paula's lip. Oh, no! Oh, nı
no, no! He wanted to grab her, to hug her, but hı
eyes flashed such hatred that he couldn't begin ı
reach out or talk to her. "Oh, my God!" he gasped, anı
tried to reach her. "Paula!"

"Stay away from me!" she sputtered, her lip swollı
and deformed, her beauty marred by the slim ribboı
of blood. "Just stay away from me."

No, no, no, it wasn't right, Tim told himself. Hı
didn't do that. He couldn't have. He wouldn't hurı
Paula. He couldn't hurt Paula, and yet he had hurı
the Badman. He wanted to cry out. No! Please, leı
him wake up and this could be all a bad dream! Hı
would never hurt her. He would never slap her. Shı
was his wife, the mother of their children. No, no, nı
he couldn't hurt her. Men who beat their wives werı
beasts. And then a wave of boyhood memories floodeı
him. No, no, no. Paula was his wife, his lover. Hı
would never do to her what his father had done to hiı
mother. He would never hit her! And yet she cowereı
away from him now, and his hand was sore, and heı
lip was bleeding.

"Stay away from me," she cried, and she ran fronı
the kitchen to the bedroom. In the bedroom, shı
closed and locked the door. It was a special lock theı
had installed so the children wouldn't interrupt theiı
lovemaking. Ruefully Paula remembered this as shı
fastened it against Tim's approach.

"Paula!" he cried outside. No, she told herself, heı
nerves ajangle, her mind striving to be clear. Shı
would not let him in. He was drunk and he was crazı
and he would hurt her—he might even have the knifeı
She must try to sleep, caged in this room, sleep anı

Ten years after the war, Tim Murphy (Don Johnson), a Vietnam vet, struggles with his memories of America's most controversial war.

Paula (Lisa Blount), Tim's young wife, loves her husband but fears her family is being torn apart by his despair.

Tim meets Luke (Robert F. Lyons), another vet, and the two men form a friendship that only those who have survived the war can understand.

Neither Tim nor Luke can forget his experiences. Tim is haunted by the memory of the friends he served with on the fire team: Rafer, Sanchez, and Badman (John Archie, Jorge Gil, and Richard Chaves).

Soldiers lived in terror, never knowing when Charlie would emerge from the jungle and strike, but hoping they'd be quick enough to catch them dead in their tracks.

Tim had been a young, innocent boy when he left for 'Nam, but he soon wore the "Black Halo."

Although the Vietnam veteran has survived the atrocities of war, he must come home and face another hell in order to reenter the world of the living in a changed America. The memories are haunting, and survival is a day-to-day challenge.

sort things out tomorrow and make plans for the future, for herself and the children.

"Paula!" Tim cried outside. It was so plaintive it broke her heart. But she had seen enough. "Go away!" she ordered. There was no threat to back up the command. It was unequivocal. "Go away!" she told her husband of a decade, now a stranger to her. "Go away!" she told the father of her children. "Go away!"

Chapter 10

Timothy Murphy awoke cramped and sore. His face rested on something cold and hard and it felt as though all the warmth had been drained from his body. He looked up, trying to focus on where he was. His eyes met his son's. Ronnie was sitting on the john watching his father wake up in the bathtub. Tim was still fully dressed. He tried to say something, but no words could express the embarrassment he felt.

"Ronnie!" Paula called. "Come on, Ronnie. Ronnie, come on." Her voice was insistent, trembling.

Ronnie flushed the toilet, jumped down, and pulled up his underpants. Like an instant replay, Tim saw it all again. The disgust, the self-loathing, the utter worthlessness he felt. He was a vile excuse for a man. How could he face her? Hitting a woman, he had long believed, was the most heinous wrong. He remembered his mother with two black eyes, staring woefully t them, the children. She stayed because of the children. She used the children as her excuse and that in turn caused Tim to feel somehow responsible. Now he had struck Paula. "Go away," she had cried through the locked bedroom door. "Leave me alone!" Unfortunately it was not a dream. A deep, dark depression set in, a sense that he couldn't escape a frightening, lonesome, futile destiny. He did not feel as though he could control his own actions.

Timothy Murphy clawed up from the bathtub, crawled across the floor, and retched into the toilet. He grabbed the cool porcelain and again and again the spasms constricted his stomach, his testicles rose up into his body, his head pounded with an intense headache, and bitter gastric juices passed through his mouth. He tried to calm the constrictions of his stomach. He stood up and drew in five slow, deep breaths. Then he looked in the mirror and began to sob. His hair stood on end, his beard was dark and scratchy, his eyes were red from puking, and his lips trembled.

"You're a mess," he cried, sick and hung over. "You're a fucking mess!" As he started out of the bathroom he heard the car door slam. "Paula!" he whispered.

He stumbled out to the living room and watched as the car backed out of the driveway with Ellen and Ronnie in the backseat. Paula didn't look back at the house as she usually did when passing up the street. Timothy Murphy put his fingers against the glass, bowed his head, and wept bitterly. All he ever wanted, all he had worked for and lived for had just departed, and he knew with profound self-hatred that he was the cause of it all.

"I've got to get this straightened out!" he whispered, his tongue thick and furry. He stumbled to the table and sat, holding his head in his hands. How did it

happen? How and why? What would happen now?
Was Paula leaving him? Could he ask her to take him
back? Should he give up drinking? Then he thought of
Luke. Fear and panic seized him as he began to blame
Luke. Luke had lost his wife and son—they weren't
coming back—and in trying to help Luke, to be his
friend, Tim was now losing his own family.

But no, he said with more honesty, no, it wasn't that
way at all. He shook his head violently. He couldn't
blame Luke. He mustn't. What had happened to Luke
had nothing to do with what happened last night.
Last night he had been reacting to that bastard Hugh
Baxter. He had lashed out at the suspicion that the
war, all the explosive, bloody violence had indeed
been in vain. Luke had saved him. That episode could
have been far worse. They could have taken the place
out, destroyed everything and everyone within sight.
He might have been arrested and jailed—maybe even
now the police were on their way with arrest warrants.

What a mess, a fucking, wretched mess. He desperately needed a drink, but he knew if he had one, it
would start all over again. He couldn't afford that. He
went to the sink and poured himself a glass of water
and drank it with an overpowering thirst. It felt cold
and cleansing going down, but suddenly nausea swept
over him and he vomited the water back into the sink.
"Fine," he muttered, rinsing out the sink. "Wonderful."

Carmen was fluttering about the counter, filling
sugar jars and napkin holders when Paula reached
The Chef's Inn. Paula bowed her head so Carmen
wouldn't see her face, and she walked quickly past.

"Morning!" Carmen called brightly. "Benny just
called. He's going to be late."

"Uh-huh," Paula said. She placed her purse below

the waitress station and primped her hair in front of the glass cabinet. Deliberately she tried not to see the bruise on her lip.

"Hey," Carmen said, "guess what? You know that guy, real cute, that always comes in here in the afternoon?" Paula said nothing. Boy meets girl, she thought, boy marries girl, they live happily ever after. "Humph," she said to herself.

Carmen continued. "Real quiet, always reads the paper, mustache, light brown hair." She smiled broadly. "Real nice buns?" She produced a folded paper from her pocket. "He left me this yesterday—'I'm not very good at small talk,'" she read, "'but I find you very attractive. Will you meet me at the bar in the Oakmont Hotel Wednesday night at nine? I know you have Wednesdays off.'" Carmen waved the note in amazement. "What should I do?"

"I really don't know," Paula said evasively. Happily ever after.

The tone in her voice caused Carmen to scowl curiously. She turned to Paula and shock widened her eyes as she saw the bruise on Paula's lip. "Where did you get that?"

"I fell," Paula said lamely, but her eyes, welling up with tears, belied her words.

"Oh, Paula, honey! Oh, you poor dear!" She clasped her arms. "Do you want to talk about it?" Paula shook her head and emitted a weak, "No."

"The bastard!" Carmen said angrily. "He hit a kid like you!"

"I'm leaving," Paula announced, astonished at the finality in those words. Then she nodded with righteous anger. "I'm leaving him flat. I can't take it anymore. I just can't take it!"

Carmen placed her arm around Paula's shoulder. "You poor kid!"

"I've tried!" Paula blurted angrily. "Honestly, I've tried! I've tried to understand, to keep everything together, to make a nice home for him. But it all goes unnoticed, unappreciated. He can go to hell! I'm taking my babies out of that house. I can't live with him anymore. I just can't take it!"

Carmen urged her on. "Go ahead! Anger is good! Get it out! Get it out, honey!" She hugged Paula, and Paula wept.

Tim showered and shaved. He heated some milk on the stove and broke pieces of toast into it and ate it slowly to settle his stomach. He was able to keep that down. Now what? Yesterday's episode had soured him on about searching for work, so he didn't care to pound the pavement again. And yet he didn't want to remain in the house. The thousand little touches Paula had set about, the flowers and photos of their wedding and of the kids, the embroidery and frilled curtains, all deepened his depression because they reminded him of how hard she tried to make his life comfortable and happy. It underscored the pain now she was gone. Would she ever come back? Could he ask her to?

Timothy Murphy left the house and walked toward the ocean. He longed to be out on the water with fresh salt breezes cleansing his mind, caressing his hair and face. It was six miles to the beach. He walked past freeways, shopping malls, old sections of town, Cuban ghettos of tacky little homes thrown haphazardly together. He passed people going to work, people with vacant, self-absorbed expressions, an entire race of mammals, clothed and sheltered, scurrying through metal and concrete mazes—overpasses, exit ramps, elevators and high-rise condos—ambitious for more, selfishly plotting on acquiring greater pleasure, money, fame, sex, power. Timothy Murphy saw the emptiness and desolation of it all now with new eyes.

Stripped bare of all dignity at boot camp, then set down in the Stone Age to sweat and hike and battle unstoppable hordes of Orientals who had no illusions about the importance and value of life, to die or else to wait until the far-off day he might return—during that time "home" had become a magic word. It did not mean a building, or even a place on the map. It meant for him the return to a state of mind, a time of innocence when he had been ignorant of the strafing and bombings, the rapes and murders and mutilations, the Hanoi sadism and Saigon coups. He wanted to reenter a teenage America of fun in the sun with his buddies and girlfriends, to celebrate his youth and the peace and harmony of that time before.

Yet he couldn't. He could never return there, and he had realized this when he got back. It was gone, that time of fun and cheer and innocence was gone forever. And so he had created around himself a quiet, peaceful, deliberately ordinary family life. Many of the GIs he knew had joined motorcycle gangs, outlaws forever after being mustered out. Some used the GI Bill to attend law or medical school. Some got heavily into crime—having seen the chaos and violence and having developed survival skills in war, crime, particularly drug smuggling, was easy, and gave the drunken rush that heightened the stakes and left a warm afterglow. Tim only wanted to be left alone. "Home" became for him a refuge in ordinary, anonymous suburbia where he owed "nothing to nobody" and could watch his children grow.

Now, he thought as he passed along through the

jangling, jostling landscape of Miami, now he was alone. He had deliberately thrust away from himself the very home where he had found such comfort and security. He had done it to himself, and that drove him mad with guilt. A grave suspicion conjured itself within him that he should seek help from someone, from a professional. Forgiveness? He thought of the sacrament of confession. Whispered words in a darkened box. Go and sin no more, my son. Forgiveness. He needed that desperately, from Paula certainly, but he needed it, he ached for it from some other quarter. He needed Paula to hold him and forgive him and tell him it would be all right.

Timothy Murphy reached the beach at last. Low clouds slid along the southern sky. He walked out on the pier where old men and young kids fished in the glistening, heaving ocean. He remembered his uncle's boat, those long sunny days on the breast of the sea trawling for marlin, when his uncle would thrill him with tales of pirates and sunken ships and untold riches of the Spanish Main. Curiously then he remembered the vast, silent, rotting Everglades, sweltering, bug-infested, suffocating in its own lust for air and sun. If only he might sit in a boat among that sprawling, crawling jungle of fish and fowl and reptiles, among the thick, rank air and muck, neither gaseous nor liquid nor solid, if he could just sit with a fishing line beneath the green scum and catch what lurked in that swamp, if he could pull a silver, shimmering fish high into the air and sun, then perhaps. . . . He shook his head and knew that he had to see Paula. What lurked beneath the green algae in that rotten swamp? Turning his back upon the ocean, he walked inland, determined to search for an answer to his problem even if he risked becoming lost in a jungle of crossed purposes and alliances.

When Tim entered the Chef's Inn, Paula's back was to him. Carmen looked up, sensing his presence, and she scowled and shook her head in rebuke. Slowly Paula turned around, and as she saw him, she dropped her eyes in sadness. She walked to the back of the restaurant and Tim followed her. Through the kitchen and the storeroom she passed, then out the back door to the parking lot.

She turned to face him, and her eyes smoldered. It was the first time Tim had seen the bruise on her lip, and the sight of it sickened him to despair. A wave of shame and disgust washed over him, and he could not speak.

"Well?" Paula said icily, her eyes glittering with hatred.

Tears welled up in Tim's eyes when he saw what he had done, and his voice caught in his throat. He didn't deserve Paula's forgiveness. He was wretched and loathsome and hung over. He turned away from those eyes that indicted him. When Paula saw his tears, her expression softened and she squinted quizzically. Tim struggled to say something. How he despised himself! How he wished he could change things, wipe away last night forever so no one would see, return to a time when they were happy and carefree. The hot tears flowed down his cheeks, and Tim turned suddenly and left her standing in the parking lot. Watching him walk away, Paula started to cry. Seeing him walk away, she realized how deeply she loved him, how much she wanted to help and nurture and care for him. God, how she loved him! If she could just get him to love himself.

As the day wore on, Paula missed him more and more and wanted to talk with him. Though Carmen insisted she should keep her vow and leave Tim, Paula knew she couldn't. Memories of their courtship flooded in around her, fond memories of tender kisses and petting and the first time ... She knew after seeing him that something deep down, farther down than she could reach, was troubling him. He had lashed out at that nameless, faceless "it" that lurked deep in his heart. If only he could land a job!

Paula's heart ached when she remembered how he'd looked in the parking lot, like a contrite little boy, shocked at what he'd done. Oh, how she wanted to hold him against her breast and comfort him. If only he were as small as Ronnie and she could hold him and comfort him and assure him that everything would be all right.

But would it? She expected to find him home when she returned at five, but he wasn't there. Frantically she called the three places he could have gone—the Statue of Liberty Bar, the Colorado Bar, and Luke's. No one had seen him. It was a sad, sickening feeling she had as the sun sank and darkness crept in and she faced her first night alone. Thankfully the children sensed the awful truth and didn't ask any questions.

"I've lived it, man, I *know*," Luke said. He seemed strangely impatient, as though he were arguing with himself. He seemed angry and accusatory, blaming Tim for what happened. "I'm still living it," he said, and he waved his arms around his apartment, its spare furnishings and unsuccessful attempts at art, "and it's no fucking fun."

Tim sat on the floor, holding his knees and brooding, blankly staring straight ahead.

"I can sympathize, Tim, but I can't be much help. I can't even sort out my own situation. My old lady . . ." He sighed. "She won't make up her mind—she wants to get back, she wants to get divorced, on again, off again, in again, out again. It's hell, man." He sighed heavily. "It's like being a fucking yo-yo."

The phone rang and startled them. "Hello," Luke said. "How are you? Oh, fine, fine. No." He looked deliberately over at Tim. "No, I haven't seen him all day. No, he never called. Sure. Right. If I hear from him, I'll have him call. Bye."

Luke sighed mightily and ran his hand through his hair. "It was Paula," he said.

"She's worried?" Tim asked.

"Yes." Luke nodded. "Worried and scared."

Tim rubbed his face with his hands. "I . . . I just don't know."

Luke shook his head. "This is the critical time, man. This is it. I can't help you on this, man, but what you do tonight and tomorrow will mean how you're going to live for the next six fucking decades. And I can't help you, man. It's something, something you have to face. I'm sorry. Want a beer?"

"No," Tim said, "no thanks."

Luke went into the kitchen, opened the refrigerator, and pulled out a can of beer. When he heard his front door close, he looked to where Tim had been sitting and saw he had left. Luke shrugged and put the beer back. He never drank alone.

Paula sat by the phone, torn between calling the places again and waiting for the phone to ring. She imagined the worst—vivid scenes of auto wrecks and blood, or else a cold, numb body pulled from the ocean by grappling hooks. She shivered when she remembered how Tim used to sit, staring blankly into the pinpoint of light on the television set, the .357 Magnum on the armrest of the chair. "Oh, please, God!" she prayed. "Make him be all right!"

Tim wanted to go home, but he couldn't. Paula was worried and scared. He wanted her to know he was all right, but he didn't want to face her. He paused at the football field where he had clowned with Luke the night before. The gate was open, so Tim went in and sat in the bleachers. Football. Combat. Capture the Flag. Games, all games. Luke had conveyed to him the greatest moment of his life, a football hero. The greatest moment of Tim's life had occurred twice—when Ellen and Ronnie were born. He, too, had been an athlete in high school, but his greatest moment was not on the gridiron. He'd had too many great moments there—breathtaking passes and eighty-yard runs—he had risen to first string on the all-city team. He had dated a cheerleader, Renée, Paula's older sister, and he ran with an energetic young crowd. Most of his buddies were now bankers and lawyers and doctors Most of the girls were married, many divorced, and a healthy number pursuing careers.

How funny life was. If only he had accepted the football scholarship up north! Instead, the fun he'd been having anchored him to Miami, to a job, until Uncle Sam sent his greeting card. While he was away, Renée had dated a law student, and she was now married to him and living in Washington. Upon his return from Southeast Asia, Timothy Murphy had taken Renée out again, but she hadn't changed from the carefree beach bunny he'd known before. Tim had preferred Paula, quiet, sensitive Paula with a sublime body and a placid, happy nature, who made love so tenderly it made his heart ache. And he had hit her! He had raised a bruise upon her lip! Wonderful. Oh, he was a dandy guy, a real first class A-1 citizen! He was trying to self-destruct, to thrust away from himself all those who loved him and could enrich his life.

The night was moonless and dark, and the warm wind blew, redolent with memories. Paula was worried. Why hurt her anymore? Why not go home, apologize and see if he might repair the breach. With his hands in his pockets, he left the football field and started home. As he turned the corner he was glad to see lights on in the house. It was comforting to know that Ronnie and Ellen were in bed, yet it saddened him, too, to realize he had caused them the least upheaval and pain.

Tim approached the house and saw Paula through the window, framed by frilly curtains. Her expression was so sad, Tim nearly broke down crying. He couldn't face her. He had caused her unknown pain and anguish. He gulped the dark, warm wind. It was quiet and dark and peaceful out here. He remembered the Everglades and he remembered a story of a monster, Grendel, sitting out in the dark, a son of Cain, envying Beowulf and the heroes within the mead hall. He felt like that monster from the swamp, looking in, unable to go inside. Beautiful Paula! He saw her again as Renée's kid sister, prancing about before him, testing out her sex appeal on her sister's date, shy and uncertain, proud and happy and filled with laughter.

Tim sat down by the swing set and idly swung a swing back and forth with his hand. How their love for each other had deepened! Then the children. They gave a purpose, a future to his life. He was startled when the door opened and Paula emerged with the garbage. Tim froze. He didn't know whether he wanted to be discovered lurking outside in the dark, nor did he want to frighten Paula. She looked about the back-yard and spied him. Unflinchingly she walked over to him. Tim raised his eyes slowly and confronted her. Instead of rebuke or hate he saw deep concern and love. He looked again, directly forward, avoiding her eyes as his tears welled up.

"I still have some dinner left if you're hungry," she said evenly, neither invitingly nor begrudgingly. She shrugged. "I haven't put it up yet."

Timothy Murphy looked ahead deliberately, gritting his teeth together so he wouldn't break down crying.

"Tim, I was worried about you. I even called around looking for you, you know? I'm just glad you came home."

Home, he thought. It was being offered to him once again, the warmth and comfort and peace he had nearly destroyed. He tried to speak. His words caught upon his tongue. "I'm so sorry," he said, the sobs racking his body, "I'm so very sorry."

"I know," she said, nodding at him.

Forgiveness and love—Tim could hardly believe the blessed joy of the forgiveness she held forth. "I . . . I've been thinking about things. I've been thinking a lot about them." He paused. "At first I thought that I could say, you know, an accident." He frowned, fighting to control his tears. He looked up and shook his head. "It was no accident."

Paula knelt down next to him. The plaintive tone to his voice saddened her terribly.

"I felt, I felt I had to lash out, I had to lash out!" He ground his fist into his palm. Then he turned, tears streaming down his face. "I'm sorry," he said, "I'm sorry for hurting you."

Paula nodded, deeply moved by his confession and apology.

"Oh, Tim," Paula said, tears running down her face. "I love you more than life itself."

Tim clasped her hand in both of his. "I've been thinking it over and over. I . . . I don't know how or what it is." He clenched his fist at his heart. "So deep, so deep inside of me." He looked up to her for understanding. "Sometimes I pray to God that He would just . ." He burst into sobs and Paula clasped him about the neck and kissed him, their tears mingling. "Oh, Paula," he said, "I need help." And they kissed and hugged while the crickets chirped in their suburban backyard and the warm dark wind blew out over the sea.

Chapter 11

She encouraged him to go to the veterans' center. It would at least help him identify his problem and perhaps show him a way to cope with it. And so Tim called and planned to attend the next Thursday night meeting. With the same reluctance he had felt as a child for the confessional or for the dentist's chair, Timothy Murphy drove down to the veterans' center.

It was a small, unprepossessing building, concrete block, flat roof, an uninspiring little place that offended him at first with its ordinariness. He had never been a joiner of clubs. He never liked to be bound by laws and rules and meetings. The notion of telling such soul-baring stories as they did at Alcoholics Anonymous or drug rehabilitation programs always made him uneasy. He had been brought up in a religion where sins were confessed privately, anonymously, whispered in the dark. He found something offensive about parading his memories and traumas before the eyes of others. But memories of 'Nam had created such a crisis in his life, he swallowed the pride he believed he was compromising, and opened the door and entered the center offices.

The interior was cluttered and dingy this night. Timothy Murphy looked around at five other men, as nervous and jumpy as he was, and tried to smile.

"Okay," Rob, the leader of the group, said to get their attention. "Let me first say welcome and congratulations to two new members, Jim and Timothy." The others clapped and welcomed them into the circle. Tim found a seat near the wall. "You have just made one of the biggest, most important decisions of your life, and we hope you're going to prove to yourself it was one of the best."

"Give them the full sales pitch, Rob," a man named Ted said. The others called out for Rob to elaborate.

"You guys are nasty tonight," he said. "Now"—he turned to Tim—"you're in for it." He grinned. The first encounter was always the most difficult. "Let me lay something out to you. This isn't going to be easy. You have already done the easy part . . . getting here. Now it's up to you."

One of the other men, Eric, mimicked the speech Rob gave to newcomers. "This is going to take a lot of work, and you're the ones who have to do it."

"Exactly," Rob smiled. Some of them chuckled. It was an odd, unsettling energy in the air, a confusion of fear and relief. "I can't promise you that this is going to be a breeze. In fact, you'll see some things that will disgust and terrify you. It's the exact opposite of easy. It's going to be hard and it's going to be painful. We return each time we meet to that Magical Mystery Tour called Viet Nam. And if you thought

it was hell the first time, just wait till we finish thi
trip."

Rob stood and circled the chairs, his voice weavin
a spell among them, patiently trying to elicit the
proper tone for their confessions.

"I'm not a magician. I'm not a witch doctor. I'm no
a shrink. If you want quick fixes and magical cures
forget it. I don't know any, any *clean* ones, that is.
Some of the men laughed.

"Besides a lot of hard work and pain, there's an
other big thing I need. I need you to be honest. You
are going to see things, terribly ugly, distorted things
sides of yourself, your personality, and things you did
that you never want to admit. For years you have
been denying these things, you have been repressing
the guilt and the horror of that time in your life, and
the wounds just won't heal. We are here to face our
selves, the self we greet when we shave each morning
the self we hope we are, and also that dark other self
the violent brooding self that we suspect and fear we
are."

Rob nodded with finality. "Other than that, welcome to the group, Tim. And let's get started. How
about the introductions?" He looked at one of the men.

"Hi, I'm Larry," the man said. "I was in Viet Nam,
sixty-seven to eight. I was with the First Air Cav." He
shrugged and turned to the next man.

"Uh, Bill West," the next one said cheerfully. "Third
Marine Division. Force Recon. I was stationed at Pleiku,
seventy to seventy-one. That's about it."

Attention passed by Rob to Charles, a handsome
young black man.

"Charles P. Harris," he said.

"Did you ever find out what the *P* stands for?" Rob
asked.

"Not exactly." Charles flashed a smile. "Anyway, stationed in Camranh Bay. Truck driving all the way to Saigon and paying tolls part of the way. You know, and that was in seventy, seventy-one, but it was a fine time in my life." He looked over to Eric. Eric was well dressed, perhaps a professional. He seemed taciturn and guarded.

"Name's Eric. Third Marines. Sixty-eight, February, when, uh, the good times used to roll." He looked to Tim. Tim nearly jumped, knowing he was next. But he swallowed hard and looked stoically ahead.

"Tim Murphy. First Cav. I Corps. Seventy to seventy-one. We did our partying out of An Khe." He looked to the next man.

"Sergeant Gerald Stanley. You can call me Jerry."

That was it for the time being, Tim knew. His nerves, strung out when he had to speak, now relaxed. Jerry was a mean-looking fellow until he smiled.

"Oh, good," Rob said.

"Ninth Infantry Division," Jerry continued, "reconnaisance. LURPS. Sixty-seven to eight."

Now Rob officially started the meeting. "By now you have all realized that there's no way we can forget 'Nam. Never. Not unless we get a lobotomy or something, and probably not even then. So we have got to learn how to *use* our experience." He held out his hands as if balancing two things. "We've got to use the negative, we've got to use the positive. And we've got to make it work for us in our daily lives. Now."

The men all looked at each other, feeling the meaning behind Rob's words. And then they began telling their stories, so many horrible stories. Collections of words that attempted to paint the perceptions of chaos and violence and evil, that attempted to reach some fountainhead of human agency, responsibility, blame, of human will—how had they done those things, why had those things been done to them, who was responsible? All the stories sought to balance actions and intention against results, to evaluate the impact of the horror and assign punishment, psychological punishment to Charlie, to the U.S. government, to a commanding officer, to an incompetent soldier or the South Vietnamese. Tim listened, but told no stories of his own.

The first night he came home from the vet center, Tim was very silent. It wasn't the angry intensity he had exhibited before. Now it was a quiet, thoughtful silence, an attitude that he might take time to think, and that nothing need be said about it. His thoughts raced. The composite horror in that room alone could fill an insane asylum. Each man had related a story of an incident that scarred him badly, perhaps permanently, had rearranged the emotional and psychological makeup so that defense mechanisms became behavior patterns. Then they illustrated how the anger and the hurt and the rage had built and built and, unable to vent itself, exploded in odd ways and ruined their lives here at home. Divorce, firings from jobs, criminal charges, alcoholism, aggressive behavior, that was the legacy of the war when translated into conduct here at home.

But no one beyond that room and that experience could understand. The screaming guitar leads and throbbing drums of rock'n'roll music pumped into the air defiantly from everywhere to deaden the silence, the drugs that took the pain away temporarily, that denied where you were and if you'd get out alive, the entire crazy melodrama played out before your very eyes with Charlie the only spectator. And Charlie must have laughed his ass off. Charlie was laughing even now. All the wreckage and the spent lives, and Charlie had won. Charlie had fucked up everyone's brain so totally that now his chaos was the only order in the jungle.

Yet there tonight Timothy Murphy learned that Charlie mustn't win, that each and every life has a future in addition to a past, and that mistakes needn't be repeated. Charlie, that grinning bastard in black pajamas, didn't deserve to win, and the fact that GIs were home, in their neighborhoods, that they weren't armed with weapons and explosives, that they couldn't blow up acres of jungle or napalm whole villages didn't mean they still weren't fighting Charlie. Every waking hour they needed to be vigilant, for Charlie came in many shapes, and always when you least expected him.

Tonight Tim felt at peace with himself. Lost before, lost in a maze of self-recrimination and self-loathing and lacking the will to keep searching, Tim had opened the right door at last. He now saw how far he had to climb out of his problems, how narrow and twisting and long was the staircase. No matter who was responsible for putting him there, he had to climb out, and at least now he knew the way out. This gave him a profound sense of relief. He watched his children play with a renewed sense of hope for the future, and when he ate the meal Paula had prepared and settled into his chair to read the paper, he was content.

He and Paula sat together holding hands that evening until after the news. Then they went to bed, and they made love silently, languorously, passionately. Paula drifted off into a sweet slumber as Tim, his hands behind his head, gazed up at the ceiling. He thought of Ronnie. Would he ever have to go off to

war? The terrible horrors he could convey to the boy,
and yet would he tell him what it was like? Ronnie
had been terribly affected by the events of the last few
days. Tim rose from his bed and tiptoed from the
bedroom to check on the children. Gingerly he pushed
open the door to their room and peered inside. Ronnie
and Ellen were sleeping soundly in the orange wash
of the nightlight. He looked closely at the boy. A beautiful, beautiful baby. It was impossible he would ever
have to go off to war. And yet, was it? He couldn't
bear to have his son living apart the way Luke's son
was. He needed the comfort of knowing his son lived
under the same roof and was protected.

Tim entered the room and wanted just to kiss his
son, to wish him pleasant dreams, but he then had a
compelling urge to hold him. Gently Tim climbed into
the bed and slowly encircled Ronnie in his arms. The
boy didn't awaken, but he murmured in his sleep. Tim
lay his head down on the pillow and drifted into a
deep sleep.

Paula awakened later and reached out for Tim. Still
the warm tingle from their lovemaking infused her,
and she wanted to hold him. She bolted upright when
she realized he wasn't there. Where could he be? Was
it a relapse? Was he prowling through the living room
armed with a knife, or else was he weeping by himself
out there?

Paula rose from the bed and tiptoed past the children's room. She went out into the kitchen and living
room. Both doors were locked, the back and the front,
and the car was parked in the driveway. Baffled by
his disappearance, then, she thought about the children. Perhaps she should check on them. She tiptoed
to their door. She peered in and was surprised to see
Tim's sleeping form in Ronnie's bed, holding the boy.

The sight caused her to smile tenderly and tears of joy welled up in her eyes. She had done the right thing and everything else had worked out. Tim was no monster, he was only mixed up and troubled, and together they could overcome any obstacle as long as his black moods didn't rob him of a sense of perspective.

In the following days, Paula did her best, too. They had joyous dinners, and they played and celebrated together as a family. It swelled her heart to discover again what a wonderful man Tim could be—warm, loving, happy, humorous, and playful. He continued to look for work, but the search now was no longer a desperate, thrashing, impatient compulsion. It was more now the well-planned canvassing of the opportunities available, with the confidence that ultimately he would find something.

To help in understanding what Tim had gone through, what he was now going through, and how she could best help him, Paula attended meetings of veterans' wives. The meetings troubled her, but she came away comforted to know that her story was far from unique, far from the worst. At first Paula only listened. She did not want to bare her soul immediately in front of a bunch of strangers.

Gladys, a pretty black girl, nervously clutched her hands in her lap. She trembled at having to face the others with her very private and very personal problem.

"He, uh," she looked down, embarrassed, "he hit me. I don't know. Four, five, six. I didn't count. Well, so we decided we'd go and get help. You know? At the VA. They're the ones who are supposed to help, right?" She grinned. "Have you ever been to a VA hospital? It's like the attic, the attic where you store things. Things you don't care about. There they store lives,

young lives, middle-aged, and old lives, stored there
because nobody wants them anymore. They're shat
tered and no longer perfect, so they're stored away
out of sight, and forgotten. We waited for three hours
for someone to see us."

The plaintive note in her voice affected the other
women. Paula sensed her helplessness and outrage at
having been hit and the inability to turn anywhere for
help.

"They finally let us see a doctor. So"—she shrugged—
"I started to tell him everything that had gone on, but
he didn't care. He just sat there reading this folder,
then he wrote on a piece of paper and handed it to us."
She broke into sobs. "It was a *prescription*! We sat
there for three hours just to get a damn prescription!"

Now Gladys wept openly. "That's when we realized,
we realized that nobody was going to help us but
ourselves. We realized that if he was going to get
better, we had to be the ones to get the cure. We *have*
to do it."

The others in the circle nodded understandingly.
Then it was Paula's turn. She cleared her throat,
looked around the circle, coughed, then spoke.

"He hit me." She looked up in panic as if someone
would say something negative about Tim. "He hurt
me." She glared again. "Once." Her eyes lurched around.
"It didn't start like that, not when we were first
married." She smiled weakly. "It just kind of came
into our lives. No . . . Wait. It really kind of started
after he was laid off. They were supposed to call him
back to the plant soon, but now with all the new
layoffs coming, it'll be pushed back another month.
Maybe," she added sarcastically, "another year or
century."

She smiled weakly again. "What are you supposed

to do till then? You scavenge around to survive. Anything. A grocery store, a gas station." She dropped her eyes. "I thought about leaving him. I . . . I didn't want to quit him, but I had to think of the children. What if he harmed them? I thought about it a lot that night. Now . . . now I know things are going to work out. Now, things are going to be fine."

"Why'd you stay?" Gladys asked. She seemed to be looking for some confirmation of her own decision.

"I . . . I don't know really. I was scared." Paula frowned. "But so was he. I . . . I felt, I felt that he needed me. He needed me to be there. I . . . I was afraid, I was afraid that . . ."

Gladys nodded with understanding. "That he might hurt himself."

"Yes!" Paula cried. "I didn't want him to hurt himself, and I saw that he might. I love him, and I couldn't let him do that."

Wendy, who was next, had left her husband. She was particularly bitter and she wrung her hands in pain. She was very pretty, ash-blond hair and blue eyes, but the worried lines on her face made her seem prematurely old. Her eyes darted and lurched about as she talked, and she chain-smoked cigarettes. The fear she emitted, though, truly bothered Paula. She wasn't coping at all.

"I know, I know I should give these cigarettes up," Wendy said this night. "I don't even like them." She paused, taking in another drag of smoke. "Sometimes I think they're the only thing that keeps me going."

The other women smiled supportively.

"He, uh, he never was violent. He never hit me. I mean, it was never anything like that. But he lied. Oh, no." She laughed with embarrassment. "Not about another . . . you know, *woman*. I doubt he dates even now. No, that wasn't the problem. But we really tried. He lied about the whole, you know, experience over there. He pretended everything was cool and easy. That's how he phrased it, cool and easy." She looked around the circle. "We tried—at least, I think we did. It sure hasn't been easy. Then maybe it's not supposed to be. But I know that I tried. I tried more than I should have. And I still don't understand what's happening."

Gladys spoke up. "It's not so easy. I mean, what have we experienced that we could ever compare it to? They all seem to be members of a fraternity with secret rules and words and rituals that we don't understand, will never understand."

"You know," Wendy continued, nervously smoking the cigarette, "I'm not really scared of him. I never have been, not what he could or might or would do to us. But I guess what I am scared about is how, well, what he might do to himself. He told me, he told me"—she clutched at her purse and wrung her hands— "he told me he'd do it someday. He'd, uh, he'd kill himself. And, and"—she began to cry—"and that *bothered* me. What do you do when someone says that?" She sobbed. "I hated what it was doing to us. But he probably lied about that, too. I only wanted life to be stable and to be secure. I wanted him to be reliable. He wasn't. So, so I had to leave. But still I loved him, and"—she fought for control, but the tears flowed down her cheeks—"so I had to leave. But . . . *still* . . . I love him, and, and . . . that's the part that really hurts." She broke down in tears. "You know" —she smiled foolishly—"sometimes I wish that love was like a faucet, you know, how you can just turn it on and off?"

She was sobbing audibly now and wiping her nose

with her finger. Paula reached into her purse, pulled out a tissue, and handed it to her. "Here you go," she said.

Wendy took it. "Thank you," she said. She wiped away her tears, then turned to the others. "I get so awfully tired of what's going on. I get so tired of watching him destroy all the wonderful things about him that I love so much." Her words rang true to all the other women, and they nodded. "My son—" She began to cry. "He idolizes him. I can see the pain in his eyes. I know that he knows that his father is . . ." She shrugged. She burst into tears, and Paula observed her, knowing too well the sick-at-heart feeling of it, and its needless, useless origin.

"I am so *tired* of it!" Wendy said. She fought to compose herself. "I am so tired of what's going on. I don't know if we'll ever get back together," she said, looking defiantly at the ring of women, wondering if she dared to say what was on her mind, then biting her lip. "And sometimes . . . I don't really care."

The despair absolutely sickened Paula. She had felt the same urge to reject Tim, to run away with the children and pretend there was a better life somewhere, someplace, and sometime else. But she had hope. She believed Tim could change, that by helping him, by not giving up, she could hold what they had together.

"I am so tired," Wendy said, "of Viet Nam!"

The next evening, Paula was doing the dishes, thinking long and hard about the difference in her attitude and the one Wendy displayed. Tim hadn't come home in time, but tonight he had called to say he would be a little late. The note of mystery in his voice had upset her, but she fed the children and now she was clean-

ing up. The front door opened, and Tim entered. Paula
murmured a silent wish that he wouldn't be drunk,
then she chided herself for feeling that way. She looked
up. He was grinning from ear to ear. Was he drunk?
Again she chided herself for that conclusion.

"You're late," she said.

Tim went over to her, threw his arms around her,
and gave her a sloppy kiss.

"What?" she asked suspiciously, and she pulled back
to search the expression on his face.

"What!" Tim said.

"What was that for?" she asked.

"What?" he said back, grinning wildly. Tim grabbed
Paula, smiled, and held her tightly.

"What is it?" she asked. "You're hiding something
from me. What is it?"

"Well," he said jokingly. "You know me so well.
Why don't you figure it out?"

Paula leaned back and scowled. Then the realization broke through days and weeks of worry and dashed
hopes, like the sun through the clouds. "Did you get a
job?" she asked anxiously.

Tim smiled and nodded. Excitedly she squealed, and
she leaped upon him the way she used to when they
first dated. "Oh! That's wonderful! Where?" Tim staggered backward and fell to the floor, Paula squirming
on top. The children came running in from their bedroom at the shriek, and they paused, laughing at the
sight of their parents sprawled on the floor.

"How much are they paying you?" she said, then
thinking better of it, she added, "Oh, I don't care!"

"They've worked out a special method of payment,"
Tim said. "I'm working at Madame Wu's sex shop."
And they both lay on the floor, laughing in rapture.

*   *   *

Even after Tim got the job in a machine shop, he kept attending meetings at the vet center. Paula, too, kept attending the wives' meetings, and shared her experiences with the other women. After one such afternoon meeting of the wives' group, Rob asked if she'd remain behind.

"How's the group going?" he asked as they walked along in the sun.

"Fine," she said, and smiled. "I'm learning."

"The other day I had a woman vet come in," he said. "And we were just talking. She said to me, 'I want to go back.' I asked her why. She said to me, 'I want to go back and find something I left there.' 'What is it you want to find?' I asked her. She said, 'The *me* I was before Viet Nam.' " He looked at Paula. "We all have something that we left there." He stopped and faced her. "Tim left something there, Paula. I know it, I know the tension and the anger and the silence. You see, I left something there, too. He left something he still values and resents losing. But he must let go eventually or it will hound him to death." Rob smiled, not wanting to alarm her. Then he grew serious. "He's not opening up at the meetings and I don't think he has any intention of opening up at all. He's faced the fact that he has a problem, but he doesn't want to figure out how to cope with it. It's frustrating me that he won't look deeper. He's too afraid, too guilt-ridden."

"Did he tell you that he got a job?" Paula offered proudly.

"No," Rob said. "I'm glad."

"Listen, Rob," Paula said hopefully, "I think everything now is going to go back to normal." She nodded. "I really do."

"Not so," he said. "Do you think it's that simple? Do

you think he can just get a nice job, fall right into the flow of society, and everything will be wonderful?"

"Well," she said, "all I know is that he didn't have this problem before he lost his job."

"He had this problem long before you were married, Paula. He's always been hurting deeper down than you or even he can see. Okay." He put up his hands. "It's frustrating to me. I mean, hey, if anybody should know that this takes time, it's me. But Tim. I see no evidence he has a desire to open up, and he's special to me. The tough cases really get to me, Paula, because they're the ones that need help the most, the ones that had the worst experiences over there in-country."

Rob smiled, and they walked on. "Do you know what the treatment is for Posttraumatic Stress Disorder? I know. I know because I've had it and I've been studying it for five years. It's called Abreaction Therapy. It's not pleasant. Tim must live again all the events until everything his mind has covered up either through guilt or shame or horror can stand out in the open and can be dealt with. It's painful, it's ugly, and it's an emotion-racking experience."

Paula looked concerned.

"Do you know how pearls are formed?" Rob asked.

Paula seemed puzzled.

"An irritating grain of sand lodges in the soft tissues of the oyster," Rob explained. "The oyster"—Rob demonstrated with his hands—"covers that grain of sand with layers of smooth material to ease the pain. Tim has been covering up some painful experience or a whole series of things he saw with a hard shell. And the shell gets bigger and bigger until it blocks out his view of the world. In order to get rid of the thing, he must cut down through the layers of defenses to the source of the irritation. Tim still seems to be building up more and more layers. He doesn't want to face anymore the fact that he needs help. Can you help me, Paula? The source of the irritation will not disappear until we can reach that grain of sand. Will you help me reach him?"

Biting her lip, tears welling in her eyes, Paula nodded. "I'll try," she said, frustrated that it wasn't over, that there wouldn't be any easy solutions. "I'll do everything I can."

The meetings upset Tim by bringing him back to Southeast Asia and forcing him to relive the horror. The terrible shock of the murders and maimings was not offset by any sense of purpose in any of the GIs who spoke at the vet center. No patriotism, no furtherance of democratic ideals, no liberation of a captive country—it was a simple intrusion, and so the hell suffered remained hell because it was not transformed by a greater good.

And some of the stories were deeply upsetting: Bill, a redhead with a childish face, talked at the fourth meeting Tim attended.

". . . We'd been out about ten days. We were checking out these hootches about four clicks from the LZ." He shrugged one shoulder as if it were a normal occurrence so far. "Nothing special. Just a bunch of fucking gook hootches. You know? You've seen them, hundreds of them, nothing special.

"Bobby, why he was my pal. We went through ITR together before we got shipped over, then we were assigned to the same unit. We both liked the Stones, man, and we danced like fools sometimes, shaking it up to get rid of the nerves." He laughed mournfully. " 'Nineteenth Nervous Breakdown,' right?" He swallowed hard.

"What about the hootches?" asked Rob, who saw him sidetracking himself from the real issue.

"We . . . we cleared out the locals . . ."

Tim, sitting toward the back, saw what was coming, and it nearly made him sick. Why couldn't these guys face it, goddamnit? He turned toward the wall as he imagined two young soldiers searching through the hootches as he and the Badman had, the Badman! He didn't want to hear Bill's story. He wanted to stand up and scream, You dumb motherfucker! What do you expect? Do you expect everyone's going to live forever?

Bill went on. "Moved them up away from the village so we could do a house check."

Tim saw Badman, arms outstretched, his mouth a sorry hole from which poured the words over and over, "Please don't leave me! Tim! Please! Please don't leave me, Tim! Don't leave me, pleeeeeease!" He bent his head down and surreptitiously rubbed the tears from his eyes. It never got any easier, he thought.

"Bobby, he goes by the door of this one hootch, and he calls out to me, 'Hey, Billy-boy, someone left their baby in here.' "

Tim broke into a sweat, and he gritted his teeth. The anguish in the air was palpable. No one dared to breathe.

Bill began to sob. "I can hear crying. I could *hear* the baby crying," he sobbed. Rob reached out and kneaded his shoulder to comfort him. "I looked at him, you know, like he was full of shit or something . . . the baby was just crying. So, Bobby goes into the hootch . . . he calls out to me, 'There's a baby . . .' Oh, *Jesus*!" Bill said, as he saw the entire event vividly, "The baby . . . the hootch . . . it was all booby-trapped!" He broke down crying.

To the rear of the group, Tim sat, tears flowing from

is eyes. He knew the keen anxiety of search-and-destroy missions, how attenuated your nerves got, how jumpy your body became, responding not to thought or logic but to fear, pure cold fear, stronger than bad-assed white lightning, lifting you up into an unimaginable awareness of your surroundings where death stared from beneath every bush, from the limbs of every tree, from every stinking little cluster of huts and smoke in the quiet ancient rain forest, while gibbons and baboons laughed from the dark heart of the jungle at those who believed they'd evolved.

And when the shit hit the fan and the fire was pouring everywhere, the teeth-gritting, eye-narrowing determination set in like rigor mortis. Badman was usually cool under fire, shouting and chattering and screaming rock'n'roll lyrics at the enemy, but deliberate and sound as he expended his ammunition. And that day, directing them not to look, not to look, then covering their escape as fire broke out along the treeline and they ran toward the Huey. There was never a warning.

Tim sat alone watching television long into the night, after "The Star-Spangled Banner" signaled the end of the broadcasting day, and the white snow flew upon the screen. Echoing in his mind were Bill's last words, over and over and over Bill sobbed, "He was just trying to help the baby!" Tim replayed the phrase many different ways: "He was *just* trying to help . . . He was just *trying* to help . . . He was just trying to *help* . . . to *help* the baby, the helpless baby," but help what? Help what? Help a baby from the return of its mother? The mother who left it in a booby-trapped hootch? What a useless excuse, he was just trying to help, a useless goddamned excuse. What difference did his intention make? The result was the same. Did the intent somehow change what happened? If he had shot the baby from outside the door and the hootch had blown up later, would that be all right? Bobby would still be alive. Bill's friend Bobby would walk away. The baby would be gone, but the baby was gone anyway. Bobby had let his guard down once, and he bought the proverbial farm. In the heat of action with fear racing like lightning bolts up and down your spine, you couldn't let your guard down once. Not even basic human compassion. If you felt anything, better plunge it down, not feel. Feeling was letting your guard down. And if you did let it down, and you did show the least compassion, the least humanity, and things did fuck up, you were haunted with the result for the rest of your life, and your motive, no matter how noble, did not excuse you one bit.

Chapter 12

Timothy Murphy hadn't seen Luke in weeks. He hadn't been drinking in bars, just a cold beer once in a while at home. He had been working around the house, repairing things and performing odd jobs with a new-found joy. He had painted the trim of the house, washed the windows, set up a workbench in the garage, fixed Ronnie's bicycle, built a new counter in the kitchen for Paula. On Saturdays now, rather than sit in the gloom of the living room watching a ball game, Tim took Paula and Ellen and Ronnie to the beach, and they flew kites and ate hot dogs and ice cream, and they laughed and romped and played. It pleased him greatly to sit upon the beach with his wife and two children and look out beyond the breakers, out over the placid, glistening sea.

It was on such a Saturday, about noontime, just before their outing that Tim mowed the lawn. Ronnie pushed a toy lawnmower behind him, and Paula watched son imitate father from the kitchen window. She had fallen madly in love with Tim again. It was as if some evil spell had been lifted, and they could all live in happiness and harmony once more.

Tim stopped, turned off the mower, and wiped his brow. "See if Mom'll get us some Kool-Aid," he said excitedly to Ronnie.

"Oh, boy!" Ronnie cried, and ran into the house. Tim scanned the lawn with satisfaction. His home was looking better. He was proud of it now, and he felt at ease in his role as suburban husband and father. What more was there to life than your family? Tim sighed.

Just then a car horn blew, interrupting his day-dream. Tim turned to see Luke pulling up in his battered Mustang. Luke jumped out dressed in a sport coat and tie.

"Whoa!" Tim called. "What's this all about?"

"This," Luke said, showing off his clothing, "is definitely *not* 'Early Lukian.' I just thought it was time to clean up my act."

"You look like a used-car salesman," Tim said, feeling the sport-coat material and laughing.

"Ah, give me a break!" Luke protested. "This is my new jacket." He thought a moment. "This is my *only* jacket. Anyway, I thought I'd drop by to say hello. Haven't seen your face since we been hustling jobs."

"You found something yet?" Tim asked.

Luke broke into a broad smile. "Looks that way. I start next week!"

"Hey, hey," Tim cried, "good news! Well, it looks like we got the Great Joker on the run. Things are turning around for both of us. What the—"

"Yeah," Luke interrupted, "but that's not the real news. I mean, what all this getup is for." He did a little dance. "Tonight's the night!" he said excitedly. "Me and my old lady!"

Tim's eyes widened with excitement and he smiled broadly. "That's great, man." He patted Luke on the shoulder.

Luke's eyes were welling up with tears of joy at Tim's congratulation. No longer with envy, now with the hope he could have a home with a lawn for his son to play in did Luke look upon Tim's home.

"Yeah," Luke said, "after I take my son to the amusement park, me and my old lady are going down to Mike Gordon's on the bay."

"Nice place," Tim said approvingly.

"Yeah, that's where we used to go when we were dating." Again Luke capered about. "Then we're going to do a little two-footing, and *then* . . ." He gestured with his hand as if he were sliding home with the winning run. He winked. Tim grabbed his shoulder and shook him in joy. "I tell you, it's just like old times. That old feeling's back."

"So, you're pulling out all the stops, huh? You're not nervous, are you?"

Luke bowed his head self-consciously. "You can tell, huh?" He nodded. "It's been quite awhile."

"Well, listen, man. You know how I feel. I hope everything goes great!"

"Thanks," Luke said. "Thanks a lot."

Tim put out his hand for the Dab handshake, a complicated ritual of hand signals ending with a masturbatory gesture. Together they performed the handshake until they got to the end, then they both paused. "No, man!" Luke laughed. "Me and the old lady, tonight!"

"Good luck!"

"All right!" Luke cried joyously. "So give me a call later, and I'll share the good news, okay?"

"Yeah." Tim nodded. "I'll do that." Sharing, that pleased him.

"Oh," Luke said, remembering. "I've got a surprise for you."

"What?"

Grinning from ear to ear, Luke proceeded around the car and with a swift kick he opened the lid to his trunk. He reached into the trunk and pulled out the upper half of the mannequin they had stolen weeks before for the "Early Lukian Art Gallery."

"Man," Tim said as Luke handed him the bald, nippleless dummy, "what am I going to do with this?"

"Bury it," Luke said. "It was great while it lasted between us." He kissed it farewell, then jumped behind his steering wheel. Bewildered at what to do with the mannequin, Tim laughed and waved goodbye to his friend.

The Timothy Murphy family spent a wonderful afternoon at the beach. Sunlight streamed down, radiating health and well-being. The crash of breakers eased Tim's mind and the forlorn squealing of gulls counterpointed the happiness and harmony he felt.

Both Ellen and Ronnie brought kites, and with a boyish joy Tim helped them get the colorful collection of paper and rags and string and sticks up into the bounteous blue sky. High they rose, like the brightest of hopes, and they fluttered and dipped up there on eddies of wind, for all to see and admire.

Tim and Paula swam out beyond the breakers. Paula had been a competitive swimmer as a girl, and Tim admired the clean slice of her arms through the waves. Since they had been coming to the beach Saturdays,

Paula's skin had turned a golden brown, and her blond hair had lightened until it was nearly white. She looked healthy, relaxed, happy, and in love. The swimming, too, had toned her muscles, and Tim said her flesh looked like that of a sleek thoroughbred. They laughed and dunked each other and they kissed as the sea rocked them up and down with its gentle motion.

Back at the towels, Tim hugged Ronnie and pointed out at fishing boats trawling on the horizon. "We'll go fishing next week," Tim said. "My uncle used to take me out on his boat when I was your age, and we'd stay out all day long." Tim scanned the sky for clouds. There were none. "We had a lot of fun." He thought, also, about fishing in the Everglades. He remembered his fishing line disappearing beneath the green scum of the water and the sense that it would pull up something old and noxious and rotten. He looked up the lines of string, then, to the kites. High above they fluttered, and the sight of them cheered him. No, they wouldn't fish in the swamp. They'd go instead upon the broad sunny breast of the sea and watch the heroic marlin leap from the waves. They'd go next week.

Home they drove as the sun was waning. The children behaved in the backseat. Paula and Tim both felt cleansed and sun-drenched. She had planned a light dinner of cold chicken and ham and salads, and she had a bottle of white table wine chilling. Usually after such a day at the beach, the tired children retired early and slept soundly. And she and Tim went to bed and enjoyed the scent of sun and coconut oil and the faint taste of salt upon each other's bodies.

The car, though, did not cooperate. At their exit from the freeway it coughed and sputtered and died. The children groaned and Paula expressed concern, but patiently Tim raised the hood, tinkered with the battery and the alternator, and soon had the car running again. All the way home it sputtered and stalled, but they finally made it.

After dinner, Tim brought his tools out to the car and tried to find the electrical short under the dashboard. For half an hour he worked unsuccessfully. He kept flicking the light switch on and off, but the bulbs remained dead. As he lay upside down in the front seat, Paula peeked in the window on the driver's side. "How's it going?" she asked.

Tim sat up, sighed, then reached over to see if the radio worked. The radio sprang alive and the station was playing golden oldies, songs from the year they had dated.

"I'll be damned," Tim said. "At least I got the radio to work." He grinned boyishly at her. Paula smiled back. She had never seen Tim so patient and calm and at peace with himself.

"Good." She took a deep breath and sighed. "It's nice and warm tonight," she said to make conversation.

Tim took the cue, reached over, and flung the door open to invite her into the front seat. The radio played sweet ballads that cast a soft glow of romantic memories.

"You know what this reminds me of?" Tim said, feeling as though he were twenty-two again.

"What?" Paula asked pertly, knowing exactly what it reminded him of.

Tim stared through the windshield as if he were seeing white lines of breakers rushing out of the black sea, and beyond, the heaving sea glittering in the moonlight. "On nights like this, we used to go to the beach and park and spark."

Paula grinned devilishly. "After you went carousing with your buddies to see if you could find anyone better!" she teased. "Do you remember that time Renée caught us?"

Tim laughed. "Oh, yeah!"

"Boy, I had one rampaging sister!"

"Especially since I stood her up to take you out."

"You know," Paula said craftily, "I always knew if I could get you to go out with me just one time, I had you!"

Tim began to tickle her, and she squirmed and squealed.

"Oh, really?" he asked. "Really, uh, pretty sure of ourselves, weren't we?"

Paula intertwined her fingers in his to stop the tickling. "Well, let's just say that I knew what you needed." She sighed, remembering the stolen kisses and the hugging and warm moments of intimacy as they explored and discovered each other so long before. "I remember all of our dates," she said fondly, and she shivered, tingling at the memory. "You used to tell me how much you loved me."

Tim grinned. "I had to say something so I could get into your pants." He said this to puncture the solemnity. It did. Playfully she hit him in the shoulder.

"It didn't work, though, did it?" Paula grinned.

"Not all the time." He laughed.

She pushed and pulled him in play. "I sure am glad I married you," she said, and her eyes were lit with desire.

"I'm glad you married me, too." He thought a moment. "You know, uh, things haven't been so—"

Paula put her finger to his lips to stop him and gently brushed her lips against his. From the radio a sweet old ballad bathed them in happy sentimentality. Tim looked into her eyes and saw the desire. He embraced her and kissed her hungrily, astonished at

the sweetness and the hunger that met his lips and
tongue. Down they slid in the front seat, moving in
unison, downward, Paula arching her back, squirming
her hips up to meet his, when—

"Mommy!" It was Ellen calling from inside the house.
"Mommy! Ronnie is flooding the bathroom!"

Abruptly they stopped kissing and looked up in
frustration.

"Right on cue!" Tim said in resignation. "Never
fails." He threw up his hands as Paula opened the
door and stepped out. "I don't know how we ever had
Ronnie!"

Tim threw his head back on the seat and watched
her walk back to the house. Her hips swung suggestively, and more suggestively, until her walk was posi-
tively obscene. She turned at the screen door, brushed
her hair over her ear, winked, and whispered, "Later!"

With renewed interest Tim returned to his work. It
would be a fine time after the kids were in bed.

Night was full upon them. The children were asleep.
Tim and Paula sat together in the living room, talking about days gone by. Tim lay his head gently in
Paula's lap. It was warm and pleasing sitting there,
the television off, and the joy at Tim's new job spilling
over into a sense of well-being they hadn't enjoyed
since Ronnie's birth.

"What do you think?" Tim asked. "Are you going to
keep going to those meetings at the vet center?"

"I don't know," Paula said. "They really helped us
through a turbulent time, and I know how effective
they can be. But, well, I might just miss the next one
and see how I feel."

"Paula," he said thoughtfully, "I think I might stop
going altogether. I'm feeling much better now, and
the pieces are coming back together with this job.

Why bring all that stuff up again? It's depressing listening to all the stories. I realize getting it all out is good, but I'd rather be here at home those evenings with you and the kids."

"I'd rather have you here." Paula smiled. "What do you say we adjourn?" and her eyes darted toward the bedroom door.

A wide grin spread across Tim's face. "Guess tonight's the night!" he said merrily.

"For what?" she asked.

"For all us folks to come on dowwwn! Luke and his old lady are together by now, too."

"So you said. That's wonderful."

"I told him I'd give him a call later." Tim sat up.

"You don't want to interrupt anything," Paula said.

"You're right. I guess I'll call him tomorrow."

Paula climbed into his lap like a little girl. "I watched you with the kids today," she said, encircling his neck with her arms. "You were wonderful flying those kites." She dropped her eyes bashfully. "I've fallen in love with you again, Tim, head over heels. There's no hope for me now." She hugged him tightly and kissed his ear. "Let's go to bed," she said. "I have a few surprises for you!"

"Haven't had an offer like that all day." He grinned. He stood up and carried her down the hall to the bedroom, depositing her on the bed.

"Let me get ready for bed," Paula said.

"I'm ready," Tim said eagerly.

"Well, you'll just have to wait," Paula protested. "I have a *surprise* for you!" She opened up a bureau drawer and pulled out a small bag, and she giggled. "I'll just be a minute," she said, and disappeared into the bathroom.

This is too good to be true, Tim thought. He suspected Paula had bought lingerie. He thought about the wholesome joy he had been feeling and the good news about Luke and his wife getting back together. Things were working out. They'd be all right. He'd promised to call Luke earlier that day. While he was waiting for Paula to get ready, maybe he could give Luke a call.

Out into the kitchen he went and he dialed the phone. It rang, and rang again, and rang again. Tim considered that maybe Luke's wife had invited him home. Yet at that very moment Luke was sitting in his only armchair in his apartment staring blankly at the phone. A supreme agony worked in his face, knotting his facial muscles, and in his right hand he held a revolver. *Ain't a problem on earth can't be solved by a loaded gun.* The old cynical maxim of his service days, yet how true. He had been sitting in the chair for an hour waiting for the courage he needed to blow his brains out. The phone was ringing. Could it be her? Could it be Wendy? He reached out to pick it up, but his hand shied away from it, as if it would spring up and sting him.

He put his hand, trembling, to his mouth. He bit his knuckle. *Ain't a problem on earth ...* But maybe it was Wendy calling. She had reconsidered. Yes, that was who it must be! Luke loathed the sniveling, groveling hope that had been sparked by the ringing phone. Almost in anger he picked it up and put the receiver to his ear, saying nothing.

"Hello?" It was Tim! Tim had caught him. What would Tim think? Luke froze. He didn't know what to say. "Luke! Hello!" Tim said cheerfully.

Luke swallowed hard, fighting back the tears. "Uh," he said raggedly, "hey, buddy!" He squeezed his eyes shut to fight back the tears.

"Hey, man, what took you so long? I was just about to hang up." Tim paused. Luke said nothing. "How'd it go?"

Luke knew he couldn't speak more than three words. He thought of saying, "Okay," but that wouldn't work. He gulped and said hoarsely, "What's the word?"

"Tell me what happened," Tim encouraged him. "How'd it go with your wife?" His voice was jaunty, but he stared into the phone suspiciously. What the hell was going on there?

Luke gulped. "The word's out," he whispered hoarsely. "Charlie's coming." The insidious whisper sent a shiver through Tim. He scowled. "Charlie's coming tonight," Luke whispered, raw terror in his voice.

"What's going on, man?" Tim demanded impatiently.

Silence. Then Luke's voice cracked and he fought for control. "She went and did it." Tim could hear that Luke had been crying. "I . . . I never thought she'd do it."

"What happened?" Tim was worried. The reference to Charlie. He could hear the Great Joker laughing. Sitting in his armchair, Luke held the phone away. His open mouth showed impossible agony as he raised the lowered pistol off the armrest.

"She . . . uh, well, she went and filed for divorce. She . . . uh, she said she met someone else. Someone, someone she can *love*." This last word was emitted like the growl of a wounded animal.

Luke slowly raised the gun to his temple. "No problem, man. No problem at all." *Ain't a problem on earth can't be solved . . .*

"Oh, mannn!" Tim said woefully. "I'm so sorry. I'm so sorry." Sorrow, so much goddamned sorrow.

Just then, Paula came out of the bathroom in a lavender negligée over a lacy "teddy" and little white slippers with her toes showing. Tim rolled his eyes at her. She motioned for him to join her. He pointed at the phone. She pointed to the bedroom. He nodded. She went into bed.

"Uh, Luke," Tim said nervously, his eyes lurching about the kitchen, "you want to have a beer? How does that sound, man, huh? Yeah, Luke, come go out with me. We'll have a couple of cold ones." His voice was coaxing, insistent, pleading.

"The word's out, man," Luke said, and the phrase sent shivers through Tim's body. The low, insidious nightmare those words conveyed! Charlie was out there, just beyond the wire, breathing, watching, and waiting, and no loud rock'n'roll, no drugs, no memories or fantasy of home would make him go away. Tim's mind raced. Distract him! he thought. Make him focus on something else, something now, something enjoyable.

"Please, Luke," he pleaded. No! Not again! "Come go out with me and have a couple of beers. Come out with me tonight, man!"

Luke's face was clenched into a knot of despair. His hand trembled holding the gun, and the steel felt cold against the skin of his temple, cold and relaxing. *Ain't a problem on earth can't be solved by a loaded gun.*

"They're at the wire, man," he whispered.

"No!" Tim cried out. "There is no wire!"

"I can see him, man," Luke groaned in fear, fear so strong and palpable it paralyzed Tim. "I can see him coming, man, coming, sneaking through the wire."

As if a cold blast of air were blowing, fear breathed out of that phone. Keep him talking! Keep him talking!

"It's over, Luke! It's all over!" Tim insisted. "You're not in 'Nam. You're *home,* man. You're *home.* You made it *home!*" Charlie! Goddamned fucking Charlie, Tim thought. How could he distract Luke long enough o get over there? The car was broken down. How? Damn t!

"The word's out," Luke whispered. "Charlie's going :o overrun us. Not again, not again."

"Oh, dear God, Luke!" Tim screamed. "Luke, please! *Please!* Listen to me!"

Sweat pouring from his forehead, his eyes and mouth wide with woe and despair, Luke made a mighty effort to control his trembling right hand, and slowly, deliberately, accurately he squeezed the trigger.

The shot shocked Tim. It was as if he was being shot at, and he was waiting to feel the rush of pain. Slowly he let the receiver slip from his hand and stared blankly ahead. Impossible! Suddenly he knew he had to get over there. The damned car! Tim dashed out of the house and sprinted up the street.

Paula heard the screen door slam, and she rose from the bed and went out to the kitchen. Seeing the phone off the hook, she picked it up and spoke into it. "Hello? Hello?" Thankfully she couldn't see into the room where her voice carried.

Tim sprinted through the darkened streets, his lungs on fire, his legs and thighs aching. He heard strafing and shelling in the wind and the screams of men as the mortars hit. He heard impossibly loud guitar licks soaring with white electric heat and the explosions that rocked the earth all about him. He heard the groaning fire tracs moving in to spray napalm over a village, and the incessant beat of the Huey pounded harder than his heart. Luke! Badman! Luke! And the image of Badman, an apparition covered in blood, eyes wild with fear, arms outstretched. "Please, Tim!" he screamed. "Please don't leave me! Tim!" The apparition screamed, reaching out, "Please don't leave me!" And Tim ran and ran, hoping to save Luke, gulping at

the warm wet wind, hoping beyond the despair he felt
that he could rescue Luke.

By the time he reached Luke's apartment, the ambulance attendants were hauling Luke's body down
the stairs on a stretcher. Red and blue lights flashed
around and around as a police officer herded a crowd
of onlookers away.

The ambulance attendants raised the stretcher up
into the vehicle and closed the door. Clean and white
and efficient, antiseptic. That's how it ended here,
Tim thought. No rats, no maggots, no rotten stench.
Not like the other time, not like that. He folded his
arms and leaned against the wall, his mind racing.
Luke. Badman. Rafer. Close friends before, now casu-
alties, taken by Charlie. Dead and gone. Oh, the blues!
Only those old blues songs with their simple lyrics
and sad pounding beat and seventh-chord melodies,
only the Delta blues could capture the pathos, could
touch the sickening ache he felt deep in the pit of his
stomach. He imagined Luke, cold, headless, stretched
out in the morgue, a tag around his toe. Oh, the blues!
Only the blues captured the sorrow and the endless
repetition of the woe. It never stopped! It never, ever
let up! He felt sick at heart, empty, filthy. What to do?
Where to go?

Timothy Murphy began to run. He wanted to see
the ocean again. He needed to be near the primal
rhythm of those waves and hear the sea moaning in
the wind. It was coming on again. The wind seemed to
rise high and screaming as he staggered through midnight Miami, down to the sea. He staggered down the
beach amid the wreckage of rock and pulverized sand
with the laughing stars burning, the palm trees groaning and sighing, and the waves, the relentless waves
heaving up, rising in the black sea into the moon,

hen spilling over and crashing in white frustration
upon the beach they sought to pull below. And he ran
and ran, trying to escape. Couples necked in hollows
scooped by the wind among the dunes, and he saw the
yell again, and his mind screamed, Don't look, Jesus,
don't look! But he couldn't help himself.

Timothy Murphy slumped down and buried his head.
He heard mortars fly above his position. The stars
danced down at him, but he couldn't escape. They
caught him wriggling by the edge of the sea. And he
remembered the screams and the groan of machinery
as the flamethrowers moved in and the phosphorus
grenades touched off each hut and white phosphorus
clouds rolled with red and yellow fire into wreaths of
black smoke, and the women, mouths red from betel
nut, as if their screaming mouths were bleeding, tear-
ing at their cheeks, clenching their jaws in angry
resentment to occupations, whatever the reason or the
army or the nation. No, no, no, he cried silently. I
can't bear it. Then he looked up and saw the sea. For
one moment he envisioned himself naked and wading
into the sea, oblivion beckoned, the cool ease of death
seemed so seductive.

But he thought of Luke. He thought of Badman's voice
that time: "Don't look, Jesus, don't look," and he had
run three miles to get there before they did so he
could rescue him before anyone else got there. It was
very important to get to Luke before anyone else did.
But Luke cheated even him, his best friend. Luke
never told about before, about before the war or his
personal relationships during the war. Luke just made
jokes and tried to laugh it off. And then Luke blew his
brains out with a gun. Big deal, Timothy Murphy
said, big goddamned deal. People died every day. They
went in their sleep. They went in front of the televi-

sion. They went on the can. They went in bed with women other than their wives. And they blew their brains out. Or else they drove their cars into garages and left them running and curled up on the front seat. Sometimes they left notes and sometimes they didn't Sometimes they were scared and sometimes they faced it heroically, as if it were the most valuable thing they had done for the rest of mankind. But they did it every day. Why should he get upset? It was just one of those things that happened every day. And yet, he said to himself as the waves crashed upon the shore, he cared. That was the difference. Luke meant something to him and he cared. And his involvement with Luke, as careful as he had been not to overextend himself, had been intense. They had shared much. He had loved Luke. He had loved Badman and they were both gone.

And then, Paula. He thought of her. He had left her alone with no explanation. He must return quickly and assure her he wasn't going to follow Luke into death. The waves held a hypnotic pull, but he wouldn't succumb. No, there was too much to live for. They couldn't understand back here, but so what? He didn't understand much of it either. He only wanted forgiveness. That's all Luke wanted, but Luke didn't know how to seek it. Tim had done all he could with Luke, and Luke had blown his brains out. So what? So, life must go on. He must go home and see Paula. Paula had looked so wonderful in that negligée, so beckoning, and Luke had been sitting that moment with a loaded pistol. He turned from the ocean, and he started the long trek homeward.

Chapter 13

t was long after midnight when Paula went outside. She wanted to see if perhaps he'd returned. Feeling cheated and used and betrayed, she wanted to confront him once and for all. She would help him, she would be sympathetic, she'd do anything to bring him back, but she would not be some doormat, some meek little woman who would tolerate anything. She had changed back into her jeans and blouse, and she stretched when she breathed in the fragrant air. Then she saw Tim crouched by the children's swing set. She walked over to him and put her hands on her hips.

"Well, there you are," she said, with a mixture of relief and impatience. "Where'd you go?" Tim stared catatonically ahead. "Oh, you're not going to talk to me?" She sat on the skyrider of the swing set. "What happened?" she asked evenly, neither critical nor supportive. "I'm not going to go back into the house. I'll

sit out here all night if that's what you want. I want
to know what happened," she insisted.

Timothy Murphy rose to his feet. "You want to
know what happened." He turned to her and sneered
and she read the sorrow in his face. It unsettled her
and it bothered her that he seemed to be trying to
scare her. She nodded and looked evenly at him. Tim
turned away and heaved a sigh. "Oh, *nothing* happened," he said sarcastically, "nothing at all. Luke
just blew his fucking brains out, that's all."

"Oh, God," Paula gasped. Her hand instinctively
went up to her mouth.

"He just talked on the phone." Tim's words had a
slow, deliberate cadence. "He talked about his wife.
He talked about 'Nam. Then he blew his brains out."
Tim paused. "When I got there, they were already
taking him away. Clean and white and antiseptic.
Just like that."

Paula stood and reached out to console him. She
remembered fondly the front seat of the car this evening, and she wanted to draw him back to that. "Oh,
Tim," she moaned, "I'm so sorry!"

Sorry, he thought, how many times must people be
sorry until they learned not to mess up their lives.
Sorrow was only an excuse. It did nothing but assure
everyone that you knew you had screwed up. "Sorry?"
he asked.

"I'm so sorry, Tim. I know how close you were."

How could she know? How could she stand there
and say that? Viciously he turned around and grabbed
her. He shook her and squinted at her and pinned her
against the swing set. "You will never, ever know how
sorry I am." The evil expression on his face terrified
her and she went limp, submissive and frightened in
his hands. "God!" he growled. "I don't want your sym-

pathy! I don't want your sorrow or your sympathy!"
His face worked with rage and disgust and sorrow. "I
don't *need* it!"

"Stop it!" she cried, beating her fists upon his chest.
"Stop it, Tim! You're scaring me!"

His eyes grew wide, impossibly wide and filled with
a horrible, hateful glare. "Scared?" he asked, his eyebrows arching, his fingers pressing into the soft, resilient flesh of her arms. "You know what scares me?"
He turned and looked around the backyard with wildly
intense eyes. His voice became quiet and soft and
slow, unworldly. "It scares me when you can't see
them, and you know, you *know* they're out there. You
know they're out there, but you can't see them. Then"
—Tim began to crouch—"then they start walking those
mortars in on you. They start bringing them in, walking them over you and nothing, *nothing* can stop them."

The jungle lay out beyond the clearing and the LZ,
an impenetrable swamp. They huddled in the bunker,
the CP a small island in the midst of steamy, rotten
decay. Charlie's at the wire. The word was out. Charlie
was coming tonight. Charlie would materialize out of
the darkness soon. With maddening certainty Tim
knew tonight was the night. They were sitting ducks.
He crouched and flared his nostrils again. Tonight
they'd be overrun.

"Please," Paula wailed plaintively. "I want to help
you, but I don't know how! I don't understand! I just
don't understand!"

Tim seemed to notice her then for the first time. He
growled and threw her weeping to the ground. "Cry!
You bitch! Cry! That'll do good. Go ahead and cry,
goddamnit. That'll solve everything. Tears. That'll make
everything better! Oh, God!" he screamed, his fists to
his temples, the maddening beat of the helicopter and

machine-gun fire exploding in his brain, "Get me out of here!" And he turned from her. "Get us out of here! All of us!" Paula lifted her hand imploringly. "Goddamnit!"

Her face was contorted with fear and sorrow. She wept uncontrollably now, and Tim bent over her.

"You don't understand." He leered at her. "None of you people understand. You're going to the prom, and we're out in the fucking bush!" He grabbed his head and screamed and sought shelter under the children's slide.

"Stop it!" Paula wept. "Please! Stop it!"

"Jeeesus!" Tim screamed, holding his temples. "Jeeesus, I can't stand the compression! Jesus, Mother of God! Make them stop, please! Oh, please!" The mortars were coming in. He could hear the shrill whine, and the explosions sent the earth flying, and men were screaming and crying, and blasts rattled his brain against the walls of his skull until his temples felt they would burst.

Paula crawled over, weeping, to touch his arm and try to bring him back to the moment. Tim seized her arm and whipped her onto the ground. "Shhh!" he said, his finger to his lips, his eyes intense, insane, his nostrils quivering in fear. "Did you hear that?" He looked to his left, then to his right to hear where it was coming from.

Charlie's coming! Charlie's at the wire! Tracers stitched across the sky, lighting up the zone of combat garishly. Sappers had breached the wire with explosives around their necks, and a dark file of little men in loose black clothing crept through the wire like shadows. Explosions rocked the earth and phosphorus grenades blew up great white and yellow billows as Jim Morrison screamed from a tape player. And someone

ehind him fired and fired, fearfully pulling the trig-
er, and more VC swarmed like shadows through the
vire.

"They're coming," he said with a sense of horror.
They're coming through the wire," he whispered. "Get
own." He grinned and looked either way. His mind
vas elevated by fear into a cool clear realm of insan-
ty. "They're coming . . . through . . . the . . . wire." He
ulled Paula as he crawled to find safety.

"Oh, Jesus," he said, "I can *smell* them. I can *smell*
hem," he whispered, "I can always smell them."

Tim grinned horribly and scanned the battlefield.
His testicles tingled and he sneered. No way. They
vouldn't take him.

"Fuck it," he spat out. "We'll waste 'em. We'll waste
em all! Rafer? Rafer? Where's the cover, man?" he
whispered. "Rafer? Where's the cover, man? My gun?
My gun!" He stared from empty hand to empty hand.
"Where's my gun?"

"No!" Paula screamed. "Stop it!"

"No!" he said, trying to hush her up, trying to shake
her off. "Where's my gun?" He rolled onto his back.

Paula climbed upon him and beat upon his chest as
hard as she could, pummeling his chest with her fists.
"No! Stop it! No! You're not going to do this! I'm not
going to let you do this to my family!" she screamed,
beating and beating, weeping uncontrollably. "You're
not in this just for yourself," she screamed. "I'm here!
Listen to me! I *love* you! I *love* you! Tim, I *love* you!"
And in frustration she slumped over him and wept,
beating still upon him.

From far away Timothy Murphy heard a voice, the
voice of Paula, Renée's little sister. Oh, that Paula
was a sweet young thing, and when he got back, when
he got HOME . . .

"I love you!" she cried, slumping over him, weeping miserably. And Timothy Murphy opened his eyes and to his astonishment saw Paula's face. She was crying though, and she was beating on his chest. Why was she crying? She shouldn't be crying. Such a sweet young thing shouldn't be crying. Was he dreaming? The thought crossed his mind that he was dead, in his coffin at the wake, and she was weeping over him demanding he rise from the dead. He tried to move his arm, and to his vast surprise, it *moved*!

"Paula?" he asked, bewildered. "Paula? Where am I?"

"Home!" she sobbed. "You're home!"

He looked around at the unfamiliar lawn furniture and swing set.

"Oh, Tim," she cried. "Oh, Tim! Oh, I love you! I love you so!" And they embraced, sobbing on the ground. He kneaded the flesh of her back to assure himself that he was indeed present under the stars in that small yard in the suburban development in Miami, Florida, United States of America, south of the mazy meandering of the Everglades, stretched out in unholy murk.

Chapter 14

The funeral was a dark, dismal affair. Funerals of suicides generally are. An American flag cloaked the coffin and a military contingent had attended to fire a salute to the departed hero. These four men, the honor guard, had pulled such duty. It was easy duty for them, compared to the duty pulled by the man in the coffin, but they despised the weeping and the sorrow and complained endlessly to each other. Yet the government had to provide a military funeral to keep up appearances. Sardonically, Tim meditated that Luke was as much a casualty as those in the caskets on the plane back to 'Frisco from Saigon.

The officer in charge of the honor guard accepted the folded flag from the two young men who'd folded it, and he turned and marched to Luke's widow Wendy and handed it to her. She accepted it with a blank face. Luke's son was by her side, looking numb and bewildered. She handed the flag to her son, then she stood, kissed the flower in her hand, and placed it on the coffin.

Paula was standing off to the side with Tim. Tim wore sunglasses to hide the redness of his eyes. When the widow stood, her veil parted somewhat, and to her shock Paula recognized Wendy of her group at the vet center. The crushing irony of it made her mind reel. All along Wendy had been talking about Luke, good, kindhearted Luke who'd made such an impression on her children. Wendy approached and recognized Paula with a bow of her head.

"Tim," she said, "I heard you were his good friend."

Tim refused to speak and looked away, his jaw set.

"Paula," Wendy said, her hand outstretched, "thank you very much for coming today."

Tim shot a look at his wife as if to question how she knew the other woman. Wendy pulled down her veil, cast a look at Tim, then turned away with the boy.

"How does she know you?" Tim asked.

"She's in my group. I didn't know, Tim. She never mentioned her husband by name."

Tim looked sternly at her. "I'll meet you at the car." He went to the graveside to pay his last respects, and while he was communing with Luke of "Early Lukian" fame who had drawn him out of so many depressions, Rob from the veterans' center approached.

"Tim," Rob said, searching for the proper tone of voice, "he didn't have to die, did he?"

Tim glared at him as if to say, "You helped put him here," then he turned on his heel and walked away.

Later that afternoon, Tim visited the football field where they had reenacted Luke's greatest moment. He sat in the bleachers and looked out, and he wept and wept. It was all so pointless. Young heroes on the ridiron, battling for their school colors, such a harmless ritual, he thought. But then war. War, the same fight for territory and for the highest score, the highest body count. He thought of Luke's medals in the frame at his apartment. Luke now was a casualty, the same as Rafer and Badman, but he'd get no medal for this one. Yeah, Luke more than Rafer or Badman had blown Charlie clean into oblivion.

He wanted to see the apartment one last time, all the lousy art and the devil-may-care bachelor furnishings. He told himself he shouldn't go, but he realized the apartment would be redecorated, the blood on the ceiling and walls covered with white shellac to kill the stain and then a coat of paint, and then life would go on as before, clean and antiseptic. On the way home, he drove into the parking lot of the apartment building. Luke's car was parked there with a bumper sticker: VIETNAM VETERAN—AND PROUD OF IT.

"Sure," Tim said, "he fucking enlisted." He climbed up the stairs and opened the unlocked door. He heard someone in the bedroom. "Hello?" he called. "Hello?"

"Yes?" came a voice, and around the corner to Tim's great surprise came Rob from the vet center.

"What are you doing here?" Tim asked in surprise. A crushing irony seemed to reveal itself to him. He stepped inside.

"I'm helping Wendy." Rob seemed embarrassed, as if caught in the act. "I'm helping pack. Where have you been?"

Tim scowled at Rob. "What? Are you the guy that's been getting into her pants or what?"

Rob frowned. "What are you talking about?"

"Well, I hope helping her out by packing is going to do better than helping her out by talking did."

Rob eyed him warily. Tim's voice was threatening and angry.

"She said she had met someone she could love." Tim walked over to Rob. Rob backed up. "Is that you, Mr. Sensitivity? Mr. Fucking Veterans' Center himself?"

"Look, man," Rob said, holding up his hand. "I'm not asking for any trouble. I'm just trying to help."

"Just leave it all here and get out."

Rob continued to pick up Luke's belongings and place them in cartons.

"Why didn't you tell us about Luke," Rob asked, trying to seem nonchalant, "that he was your friend?"

Tim was on the verge of exploding. "Who the fuck do you think you are—God?" He picked up the frame with Luke's medals in it. "All this, this *bullshit*. You're as phony as a fucking recruiting officer." He hurled it into the wall. The frame crashed and broke and the hero's medals sprinkled to the floor.

"So, that's the way it's going to be. You're just going to hide, hide like Luke."

"Yeah, sure, so you can steal my old lady, too! No way, you son of a bitch. I'm going to be there always, cause I'm a mean motherfucker, so don't you forget it."

Rob crossed the room and picked up the pieces of glass and the medals. "I thought Luke would have liked his son to have these." He looked up. "I guess you see it differently."

"Oh, fuck you! How'd you do it with his old lady, man? Did you tell her first that Luke was just a little messed up, then slowly suggest his problems were maybe a little more severe? Oh, and then you'd comfort her. The kid. Yes, take care of the kid. Make sure he gets the medals. His old man's long and silent underground, but at least the kid has medals." Tim sneered at him. "How long are you going to be staying with Wendy?"

"I'm not with her, Tim. I have never associated with a veteran's wife. It's unethical. But I can understand your anger."

"Oh." Tim laughed loudly. "You clean apartments on the side?"

Quietly, sternly, Rob stared at Tim. "I do whatever I can to help, including taking abuse from you. You didn't know Luke too well, friend. I did. He was lost a long time ago, before you ever appeared on the scene. He came to the center, and he sat at the meetings, but he wouldn't open up."

"I never had a problem getting him to talk."

"Neither did we, but it was all lies. It was all lies how he'd say things were getting better, that his wife would be back soon and they'd be happy. First it was his art he was going to sell. Then he was to make a fortune selling dictionaries. Then he got in with a rock group as a singer and they were going to cut an album. Lies, all lies. And meanwhile Wendy was waiting for him day and night, waiting to straighten out his head so he'd be dependable and honest. The worst thing, though"—Rob fixed Tim with a sidelong glance—"is that he lied to himself."

"You're so full of bullshit, man! You sit in your fucking veterans' center like God Almighty judging everyone, listening to their fucking confessions, doling out forgiveness like candy. You want everyone to come crawling to you because it makes you feel powerful." Again he sneered. "You're a fucking maggot."

Rob drew himself up to his full height, and he smiled at Timothy Murphy. "I saw action, Tim, you forget. I was a mess. This"—he waved his hands around at the packing cartons—"this is how I cope. I lost my wife

and three kids. They're back in Virginia. You, you
and Paula and all the rest are all I have to live for,
and if I can help you, then it's somehow better for me.
It's okay."

Tim stared at him, drawing in what he had said and
trying to adjust his thoughts accordingly.

"So, I hope you make it to the next meeting," Rob
concluded. And he turned away and began packing
again. Tim boxed the room with his eyes. Already the
landlord's painters had patched the holes in the wall
from the bullet, and as soon as the plaster was dry,
they'd spread the four gallons of paint by the threadbare sofa. Then they'd rent the place out again. Everything tidy and clean and antiseptic. That was how
it was to die here at home.

Tim turned from the apartment and drove home. He
didn't want to go in just yet. He sat on the kids' swing
set, swinging back and forth. He looked through the
window and watched Paula clear the table and place
the dishes into the sink. He ached so very deeply. He
longed to walk again to the sea and to look out and
feel how petty and small his own problems must be in
the vast scheme of things. He longed to get very very
drunk to toast Luke's uncharted journey into the unknown. He shied away from reentering his own home
because he felt so ill at ease. Now he was sobbing, and
he did not know why. Luke? Badman? His own unlim-
ited sorrow? His chest heaved with sobs, and the tears
scalded down his cheeks. Lies. Rob had seen through
Luke's lies. Luke had wished things would happen,
like Saturday, hoping his wife would take him back,
lying to himself and to Tim. Lies were no good. Only
truth could do it, could purge the awful guilt and
pain.

"I've got to put an end to this once and for all," he

aid to himself, and he thought of the grisly way
Luke had chosen. "I've got to." Instead of entering the
house then, he got back in the car, and drove for
fifteen or twenty minutes until the car, almost under
its own power, parked in the lot of the veterans' center. Tim saw a light on, and he didn't know whether
to be relieved or afraid. After the terrible things he
had said to Rob, he wondered if he would be welcome.
He knocked and heard Rob say, "Come in."

Tim entered the dim veterans' center hesitantly. He
didn't want to be too brash. He wondered if he should
apologize. He looked at Rob, and Rob twirled a pencil
in his hands. Saying not a word, Rob motioned him to
a seat.

Timothy Murphy sat and looked long and hard at
Rob. Rob's handling of his rage at Luke's apartment
had engendered trust. Rob looked as if he had been
expecting him tonight. He did not know how to begin,
but he knew what had to be said. Tim stood and went
to a map of Southeast Asia on the wall, the great *S* of
Viet Nam rearing high like a cobra.

"Every day," he said, "you could feel the seconds,
the minutes. Fear everywhere. Everything around you
meant something. You felt and heard everything. The
air, the sun shining on your face, the lush shades of
green, the slow primitive pace of the people, nothing
was lost to you there." He turned to Rob. "Funny, isn't
it? There's death all around you and you've never felt
more alive in your life."

Slowly, deliberately Tim crossed the room to a chair
in front of Rob's desk.

"When someone bought it, it hurt. But you just kind
of, kind of tried to laugh it off, turn your back on it."
He looked down into his empty hands. Then he looked
up. "You'd say it was his turn. Hell with it. You even

start to believe that you're invincible. Nothing is going to get you. Those sons of bitches haven't invented th
bullet that'll get you. You grasp at things so it will b
certain, it'll be all right. I wore a black headband.
called it my Black Halo. I believed as long as I wore i
through that Valley of Death, I'd fear no evil. Ther
was a village," he said, not changing the pace of hi
speech but changing the tone. "Intelligence said i
was an NVA stopover point. Maybe even a POW camp.'
He paused.

"We went in before sunrise, landing a few clicks
from the village. It was a two-company operation. Us
from the southeast, Alpha Company from the north
and west."

Again he saw it vividly, as he'd seen that day in his
dreams for twelve years. Himself, Rafer, Sanchez, and
the Badman stealthily advancing through the bush.
The rustling of leaves, the crying of birds and monkeys mocked them with the threat of death as they
held their M-16s at the ready and stalked Charlie.

The village had only about seven hootches. Some
fires, recently put out, still smoked and smoldered,
but there was nothing stirring, not even a chicken or
a dog. Slowly, methodically they inspected the huts,
trying the doors and the window flaps with the barrels of their weapons, waiting in tangible fear for the
first explosion that would send them all diving for
cover.

"My fire team was just entering the village area,"
Tim said. "It was myself, Sanchez, Rafer . . .

"Cautiously we inspected all the huts, and when
that was finished, Sanchez and Rafer relaxed in the
center of the village.

" 'Shit!' Sanchez said. 'Man,' he complained, 'I told
you guys Charlie had booked on out of here.'

" 'Yeah,' Rafer said sardonically, 'he knows I got three days to go, and I'm kicking ass.'

" 'Fucking A,' Sanchez said. He kicked the side of a hootch. Then we heard a low buzzing sound.

" 'Hey,' Rafer asked, 'what's that sound?'

" 'Something's buzzing,' I said.

"Rafer pointed to the edge of the village where the sound seemed to be coming from. 'Fucking looks like a well,' Sanchez said.

" 'Let's check it out,' Rafer said.

"They both walked over to the well covered with corrugated steel, and they readied themselves to lift it up. I followed behind them.

" 'Stay away from there, man!' Badman called to us. 'Don't open it!'

"Then Sanchez and Rafer threw off the lid of the well. 'Oh, mannnnnn!' Rafer groaned. With my weapon at the ready, I advanced to the edge of the hole, fearing what I'd see inside, knowing I shouldn't look. Sanchez and Rafer stood horrified, unable to move. I looked up and over, into the well, and saw bodies, bodies in green uniforms, bodies with silver dog tags shining up at me, and across the bodies scurried fat brown furry rats. And worms slid in and out and the smell of rotten flesh!" He winced. "The stench. I couldn't believe it!"

" 'Man,' the Badman called, 'I *told* you to stay away from there.' Flies, impossible hordes of flies, and maggots crawling over the bodies in the well. The bodies were those of American prisoners of war, and each had his hands tied together and a small red hole in the back of his head. The rats were gorging themselves, leaping from body to body.

" 'Oh, no!' Sanchez groaned. 'You motherfuckers!' He opened fire on the rats. I just stared down, watch-

ing the bullets riddle the corpses and the rats burrow
for cover.

"It was then that we drew fire from the edge of the
jungle. Rafer flew up and landed by my side. I jumped
to the other side of the well, behind a pile of dirt. We
started to return fire.

" 'Let's go!' Badman screamed, and he opened fire
and dashed for the cover with us. They poured it on,
those snipers from the trees. We were pinned down
real bad, and all they had to do was outflank us. I
tried to pull Rafer's body back with us, but Badman
stopped me. 'He's gone, man, he's gone.' Fear showed
in every line of his face, but I swear he was the coolest
in a firefight. He looked up, and we all heard at that
moment the Huey. Swing low, sweet chariot! Never
heard anything sound better than the rotors of that
Huey. Then mortar shells began walking in on us.

" 'They're not going to wait all day for us,' Badman
cried. 'Let's get out of here. *Didi mou!*' And he was off
and running. I looked at Sanchez and he looked at me,
and we jumped and ran. The mortar came closer and
closer, and we ran up the path, shells exploding all
around us. Badman stopped to see if we were coming,
then he covered our flight, spraying the jungle with
fire as we broke into the clearing.

"I looked up and saw that Huey coming in. Like a
fucking angel of God it swept in and hovered over the
swale of elephant grass. Sanchez was screaming and
waving, and I was calling to Badman, and he was still
firing, motioning us to get going, to get aboard when a
mortar shell exploded so near the compression knocked
out my breath and sent me spinning up in the air,
over and over and over, until I landed on my shoulder
and thought my back was broken. I tried to move my
arm, because I thought I was paralyzed, but it moved.

I looked and the Huey was hovering just out of range of the mortars, but the VC were walking their way toward it. Frantically, the gunner was waving us aboard. 'Come on! Come on!' he screamed. I tried to stand up, and miraculously my legs worked. Sanchez was screaming, covered in blood, screaming, 'Tim! Please don't leave me here! The rats! The fucking rats! Please don't leave me!' I crawled over to him and screamed, 'No way I'm leaving you, man!' And I helped him to his feet. His left arm was a tangle of bone and muscle, and his leg was all fucked up so he had to limp along. But I carried him a hundred fucking yards all the while the ground was heaving and the fire poured in.

"The gunner of the ship kept dumping fire into the jungle, but he fired in vain. They were entrenched and hidden, and adjusting their sights to blow that ship clean out of the air.

" 'Get on!' the gunner screamed. 'Come on, man!' And he was scared shitless. 'Get the fuck up here!' I tried to lift Sanchez up, but he slumped back because of his arm. The pilot lowered the Huey a bit, and the gunner reached down and I pushed up on Sanchez's ass and they lifted him up. Then I grabbed the net, and I hauled myself off the ground. 'Let's split,' the gunner cried.

" 'No, man, no!' I screamed. 'There's one more of us!' The pilot hovered about ten feet above the grass. Then a mortar exploded only thirty meters away.

" 'We're out of here!' The pilot screamed above the roar, and I scanned the brush, and I saw Badman, covered with blood, his arms outstretched.

" 'No, no, wait, man!' I screamed to the pilot. 'Wait for Badman.' I grabbed the gunner and shook him. 'Wait! Goddamnit!' And I looked back, and the Badman

had his arms outstretched. And the rotors beat so loud
in my mind. A mortar exploded only feet from us and
the concussion rocked the Huey nearly out of the air.

" 'Please,' I saw Badman say, 'please don't leave
me. Please, Tim.' I saw his mouth working, pleading,
his arms outstretched. 'Please don't leave me!' And he
tried to run toward us, but he fell down.

" 'There he is,' I cried. 'He's crawling, man. He's
alive.' That jockey in the cockpit maneuvered quickly,
and my stomach spun dizzily, and a shell exploded
right where we had been hovering.

" 'Get the fuck out of here!' the gunner hollered, his
eyes wide with fear. He grabbed me, or I swear I
would have jumped out to get Badman. 'We've got to
go back and get him!' I shouted, and the rats had
scurried all over the corpses in that pit. 'Look, I can see
him crawling, man. He's alive. Please, sweet Jesus!' I
was crying like a kid as that Huey rose up. And I
pointed down to the grass where Badman was kneel-
ing, praying for us to go back, his arms out, pleading
to me. 'Don't leave me, Tim! Please don't leave me!'

"And another shell, man, another fucking mortar
shell convinced our pilot it was suicide to stay. I was
at the door, screaming, pounding on the gunner's chest.
It seemed we'd been hovering there a fucking hour.

" 'Please don't let him die, please,' I cried. 'I saw the
well, man! I know what they'll do to him. I saw the
well.' And the gunner shoved me out of the way to
reach Sanchez. And I was sick because I knew what I
had to do. In that one, precise, keen, clear instant I
knew. I knew there was no choice, no fucking choice
on this earth, and I was screaming to the pilot, to the
gunner, to anyone who would listen, 'Please don't let
him die,' and the Badman was struggling to his feet,
imploring me, praying for me to save him. 'Please

don't leave me, please, Tim.' And I reached over to the gun at the open door, and I said quietly to myself, 'Please forgive me, Badman,' and I took careful aim. It's important to take careful aim. The ship even then was pulling away, so I carefully started to Badman's left and I sprayed a line of bullets, and Badman's eyes started out of his head, and he left the ground and flew backward into the grass, and we were up and out of there. I wanted to turn the gun on the pilot and the gunner, but the gunner came and put his arms around me and hugged me, saying, 'You had no choice, you had no choice.' Badman was dead. Missing in action. And I was decorated as a hero for saving Sanchez."

There was silence in the room of the outreach center, and the anguish still lingering in the air was palpable. Timothy Murphy was sobbing in his chair. "I'm sorry!" he said over and over, "I'm sorry."

"I know," Rob said, his hands folded and held to his pursed lips. "I know."

"He's still with me, every fucking hour of the day and night," Tim moaned. "We were best friends. You don't know how he looked up to me, how I wanted to protect him. Like me and Luke. And, and . . . and I killed him! And I want him to understand! I want him to forgive me, to say it's okay," Tim wept. "But I don't know where he is."

"It's all right," Rob said, reaching out, clasping Tim's arm. "It'll be all right now."

"Oh." Tim shuddered, "Goddamn! Goddamn that evil place!" And he cast a spiteful look toward the map on the wall. "And yet I know the evil's within me. I know it." He beat his breast. "And I can't do anything about it. And that's what it's been every fucking day since then."

Timothy Murphy fought for control. He dried his

eyes, and he looked with resentment at Rob. He wanted Rob to say something so he could react angrily and storm from the building, but Rob simply said: "You've never told Paula?"

He shook his head no.

"Maybe you should open up to her. She needs to understand, Tim. She's a remarkable woman. You're very lucky."

Tim stood and turned away from him. "Thanks for listening," he said over his shoulder.

"Sure," Rob said. "And Tim, see if you can come to Thursday's meeting. It'll help you greatly now that you've opened up." Tim turned around and Rob winked at him. "Be there or be square."

Despite his saddened state, Timothy Murphy flashed Rob a smile and he left the center. He knew he needed no more meetings, at least at the center. He knew now he needed forgiveness, forgiveness from Paula and from the Badman's family. Only forgiveness would remove the mark of Cain that encircled his head like the Black Halo.

He left the veterans' center and drove toward home. He wondered mightily if he had done the right thing. Was it all right to relate that story? What had Rob tried to elicit from him, and why? He had grave misgivings, alternating with periods of elation that reassured him he had done the right thing. Luke and Badman. The one death he caused, the other he had nothing to do with. The one he felt responsible for, even though in the heat of battle; the other he could never feel responsible for because it was out of his hands, Luke had simply slipped out of his hands. Personal responsibility—how far did it extend? Only so far, he knew now, and then you couldn't feel that you were to blame.

That evening, Tim told Paula the story he had related to Rob at the vet center. He fleshed out the story with more details about how close he and Badman had become, what they meant to each other, and he wept describing the shooting during the firefight.

"He looked up to me!" Tim said intently. "He *needed* me! And I killed him."

"But you had no choice," Paula said, frowning. "You had absolutely no choice in the world."

"I can see him calling out, Paula. He's covered with blood, pleading, 'Tim, please don't leave me! Please, please don't leave me!' and so I pick up the weapon, and I start carefully to his left—"

"Stop, Tim . . ." Paula said gently. She touched his arm. "Don't think about it. It's over. It's over and you're home." She embraced him and kissed him. "I love you more than I can ever say, more than you'll ever know. And now, knowing what you carried down deep inside for so many years, I love you for your courage in trying to face it alone." She shuddered. "I cannot even imagine how you must have suffered all these years with the guilt and the buried memories!" She smiled gently. "But why didn't you tell me? You could have told me, Tim. I would have understood."

"I never wanted anyone to know. I never wanted to admit it to anyone, ever. What happened over there happened over there. I did not want to bring it back."

"But you couldn't help bringing it home. And you have suffered for so long! Oh, Tim, I'm so very sorry, sorry for you and for all the suffering and for all the pain the war caused! I'm so sorry you lost him . . . and now Luke. So much death. Such a waste." She held his hands and her eyes brightened. "And yet, you men who made it back, you possess something nobody has who didn't go over."

Tim smiled curiously.

"You know the horrors of warfare, and so you know how it must never, ever be repeated. So far, every generation has had to learn that, Tim. But just maybe you men have learned it for us once and for all. And perhaps with what you know, and how you use it, Ronnie will never have to go to war."

"Ah, Paula," he said. "You find the silver lining in every dark cloud."

"But you are not alone!" she said. "Badman is gone and Luke is gone, but there are thousands upon thousands of veterans of Viet Nam who share your experience, who came back to the same troubles you have had, and there's a bond that unites you. You are not alone, Tim. It's just, it's just that because the war seemed unpopular, few wanted to admit they had participated. But it shouldn't be that way! It mustn't! You did nothing wrong. Your country asked you to fight, and you did your duty. You should be proud of that no matter what the result of the war. In the final balance it wasn't the men who fought that lost the war, it was the politicians who dragged it on for so long and never decided how to cope diplomatically with the problems the war brought. Poor Luke." Paula sighed. "He chose to go it alone, and he couldn't bear all the horror and the guilt. Many can't cope. Slowly he destroyed his marriage, his family, and then himself. But there are many, many fellows out there who are trying, who are making it, who have turned that hell and bloodshed into something positive, something meaningful and positive for themselves, their families, and their communities. Now that I know, Tim, I can help you!"

"You are a wonder," Tim said to her. Her words made tremendous sense. He kissed her, and as she responded with passion, he felt the warm delight of her sympathy, her forgiveness, her understanding. It was out, it was all out at last, and Paula understood.

They made love slowly that night, each with a new appreciation of the other—Paula that he had been through such horror, had been forced to make such a decision, and then had borne the guilt deeply buried for so long; and Tim that she had remained at his side, guiding him, helping him toward self-discovery and understanding.

In the ensuing weeks, Tim came to see Badman's death not as his personal murderous act but as another coincidence of the war. If Badman had kept up with them . . . if the VC along the treeline had been shelled . . . if Sanchez hadn't drawn their fire . . . a hundred if's, and Tim saw with a clarity he had never before possessed that he just as easily could have been in Badman's situation, and that he would have preferred death to the torture and the horrors of that well of bodies. Badman's death was a product of the war, not his personal responsibility.

Tim saw, too, that Luke's death provided a keen insight into purging the guilt and horror. Honesty with yourself opened lines of communication with your family and friends, connected you to others and allowed you to share. The give and take, the shouldering of each other's burdens, the helping hand and warm smile of understanding, that was the essence of life. The hiding, repressing, denying, cutting yourself off from others—that brought out all the dark energies eventually in twisted, monstrous shapes.

For the next three weeks Tim considered himself the happiest man on earth. After he had labored so long to shoulder his burden alone, he felt the lightness and the joy now that it was lifted, and he saw ordinary objects around him with extraordinary insight. Yes, he had made it back, and the realization of that simple fact imbued his world with happiness and light. The dark night of the soul had passed, and he felt tempered and wiser. He possessed the courage now to tackle any problem, for he had seen the worst and he had come back from the brink. He loved life, he decided, and he came to see by watching Paula and the children, by thinking out the ramifications of his deed, that what he had needed all along was simple forgiveness. Not the forgiveness of a religion, not the forgiveness of a nation. They were vague forms of forgiveness, and so inadequate. Paula had showed him the way. The forgiveness must be personal and intimate. He had wanted Badman's forgiveness, the assurance that in that situation he had done the right thing. But Badman was dead. He had been left upon a battlefield half a world away. And so Tim had despaired. Now he saw that he himself could provide the forgiveness. Once he was able to admit the deed openly, painfully but courageously, the forgiveness flowed.

Rob visited him one day. "We haven't seen you in weeks," he said.

Tim smiled. "Yeah. I've been spending a lot of time with my family."

"When are you going to come down for a visit?"

"Oh, soon. Soon."

"You know, Tim, that night, the night after Luke's funeral, I kept the vet center open because I knew you'd be in."

"Uh, yeah," Tim said. "I've been meaning to apologize for what I said in Luke's apartment. I was very angry and I was looking for a target to vent it upon."

Rob smiled. "That was the key, Tim. I knew when
ou exploded there that you were getting close to
eaching out, to relating what had been troubling you.
And so I just went to the vet center and waited."

Tim smiled. "It's that predictable?"

"You must remember, Tim, that I went through it
myself. I know. And that's why I've come here tonight. I want you to come to another meeting, just one
f that's all you want to attend. But it's important for
you to tell your story to other vets. What do you say?
Will you come tomorrow night?"

Tim thought for a moment. So far he had only told
the story to Rob and to Paula. Did he need to tell it to
the others? He nodded. "Sure," he said.

"It'll help you, and it'll help them," Rob said.

"I'll be there."

The next night, Rob turned to him first. Unflinchingly, with all eyes upon him, with all heads nodding as he described scenes familiar to them all, Tim
again relived the hell of the bodies gnawed by rats, of
the firefight, of the Huey lifting into the air, and
Badman's death. Again he wept in sorrow. So poi-
gnant was his story that the others rose up and walked
across the room and huddled about Tim in a communal embrace. And from their embrace Tim drew
strength, and he accepted their sympathy and their
understanding now, for he had come to terms with the
deed at last.

Chapter 15

Timothy Murphy booked a flight to St. Croix for Paula and himself. They would stay an entire week, a second honeymoon. In the luxurious Hamilton House in Christiansted they ate delicious meals slowly. They ambled along the bay where sailing ships rode at anchor. They made love in their spacious hotel room. They shopped for souvenirs. They listened at night to the steel-drum bands. They snorkeled in the coral reef and were awed at the color of the fish—pink and bronze and lilac and moon silver and indigo and sapphire. The mysterious tang of nutmeg and cayenne hung in the air, laced with fragrant smoke from charcoal braziers. At sunset they watched the fishermen sail out to sea, their hurricane lamps greenish upon the water, and they watched others return from a day upon the sea, unload their catch, and hang up their nets.

One afternoon Tim hired bicycles, and they rode up nto the mountain passes. The great slumbering cone)f the volcano rose to the sky, and near a dilapidated staircase reaching up into the jungle, they ate a picnic lunch. "Let's explore," Tim said with a boyish sense of excitement.

"Aren't you afraid?" Paula asked.

"Of what?"

"I don't know," she said. "Of voodoo?"

Tim laughed and pulled her up, and they trailed up a path through the jungle. They marveled at enormous ferns, at vines afire with red blossoms that twined up giant palms. They were awed at green explosions of *balisiers*, at the pliant, quivering bamboo, and for her Tim picked orchids. Above them in the trees parrots screamed, their blue and scarlet and lime-green plumage flashing in the shadows of the jungle canopy.

They came at last to a clearing where a bed of moss lay in a single ray of sunshine. Giant ferns towered above that bed of moss, and beyond the bending palm trees, the ancient cone of the volcano rose in fainter shades of blue.

"Let's rest a moment," Tim said, and he led Paula through the ferns to the bed of moss. Though she was somewhat shy and she looked about for insects and snakes, she went with him, and they lay together looking up at the extinct cone of the volcano. "Just think how once the hot lava poured from there," Tim mused, "and the ash and flame erupted into the sky. You'd never know it now. How the rock must have boiled, judging by the hardened rivers of lava! And how it must have vaulted and spilled from the wound in the earth, down to the seabed to form this tiny island. You'd never know it now."

Paula rested her head upon his breast. She had worn a simple white dress and a Panama hat. Tim brushed her hair aside and looked lovingly down into her eyes. "Oh, Paula," he said, "I feel so clean. I feel as though . . . as though we are Adam and Eve"—he waved his arm about the jungle—"and that this is Eden." He kissed her passionately, and she tangled her fingers in his hair. They made love then, naked upon the moss, and as they lay there, spent and happy and sated, a thundershower erupted and drenched them. But they did not rush into their clothes and run down through the jungle to their bicycles. No, they lay naked in the rain, upon the bed of moss, allowing the rain to fall upon their faces, their limbs, their breasts and genitals, catching it in their mouths, laughing and kissing and sputtering, not bothering to dress, laughing as though it were the dawn of time and they were two innocents called upon to people the world with a new race. The silver rain fell in sheets, cleansing the palm trees, the vines, the ferns, and the moss. Green, deep hues of green startled them as the rain let up, and when the rags of cloud parted, they lay back, wet and happy, gazing up at the faint and mysterious violet of the sleeping volcano until the sun lanced out from behind the clouds and lit it in stark relief a deep and pleasing blue.

"Oh, Paula, we are so lucky." He sighed, gazing up at the massive mountain.

"I love you, Tim," she whispered.

When they returned to Miami, Paula found a new job, working as a receptionist in an obstetrician's office. She loved the job, for it allowed her to fuss and care for expectant young mothers, to answer some of their questions, and get somehow involved in their ives. Tim's job allowed him two weeks of vacation, ind in the fall he packed up the family and drove iorthward on a pilgrimage.

Up through the Blue Ridge Mountains of Virginia hey drove, awed by the majestic scenery and the ittle hamlets all through the area where the Civil War had once raged. Into Pennsylvania they proceeded, ind to the coal-mining town of Scranton.

"I'm Timothy Murphy," Tim spoke into the phone :he night before they reached Scranton. "I was Eric's good friend in Viet Nam. I'll be passing through Scranton with my family, and I'd like to visit you."

"Sure, by all means," Badman's father had said. "Don't forget us! We'd love to see you on your trip."

The Badman had told him about great black heaps of slag surrounding the city, yet all appeared lush and green. A replanting drive had begun, and the coal companies were covering the slag heaps with sod and making them into parks. The leaves of the trees were burnished, tinged with red, and the overcast sky lent a solemnity to the day.

It was a small frame house that needed painting located up a dead-end street. The grimy coal dust clung to the storefronts, the homes, the lawns and gave everything a dour, dismal cast.

Mr. Badowsky, a short, bald, white-haired man with a chronic miner's cough, brightened when they arrived. Mrs. Badowsky, a plump matronly woman in a print dress, seemed very sad. She hardly spoke. Mr. Badowsky offered Tim a beer, and they sat in the living room hung with heavy curtains, a crucifix on each wall, and they reminisced.

"He wrote often of you," Mr. Badowsky said. For their visit he had brought out a box of letters that

Badman had sent from Khe Sanh. "He considered yo
his best friend."

"And he was mine," Tim said. "He was a great guy
and we were making plans to go into business to
gether after the war."

"Yes," Mr. Badowsky said. He reached under a ta
ble and pulled out the box of letters. "He wrote u
about that, about a pleasure boat you were plannin
for Miami. He was such a good kid," Badman's fathe
said. "I didn't want him to be following me down int
the mines, so I encouraged him." He began to cough.

Mrs. Badowsky's eyes were red and she produced a
handkerchief and blew her nose.

"So what brings you this far north, son?" the patri
arch asked.

"We're going to Washington, to the Viet Nam Me
morial. I've got to see it," Tim said. "I've read so muc
about it."

"I know you were his best friend," Mrs. Badowsky
said then. "Would you, would you do me a favor?"

"Anything," Tim said.

"Eric, well he owned a red Chevrolet convertibl
that he prized above all his other possessions." She
handed Tim a picture of the Badman standing by the
convertible with a beautiful young redhead. "That's
Sally . . . she married a teacher and moved to Ohio,'
Mrs. Badowsky explained. "Would you look for hi
name on the memorial and leave this picture nearby?'

"Of course," Tim said. "Of course."

They talked for two hours, the children behaving
themselves in the hushed, darkened living room. Then
they left.

As they drove toward Washington, Tim was thoughtful. Finally Paula asked, "What is it, Tim?"

"It's just so sad," Tim said. "I wanted to visit the Badman's house and tell his parents, confess to his parents what happened, how they lost their son." He set his jaw. "But when I saw them, how proud his dad is that Badman died for his country, how much they suffered when not even his body was returned, I knew I couldn't do it. I thought I needed to confess it to them, but I see now that would have been a mistake. I did start to tell his father," Tim said. "We walked up to look at the Badman's room. I told him that his son died trying to save our lives.

" 'He considered you his best friend,' Mr. Badowsky said, as if that was all the explanation in the world that was needed."

"That's all you need," Paula agreed. She held his hand. "That's all you and they and anyone else needs. . . ." And she smiled sweetly.

They stayed outside of Washington and entered on a Sunday to avoid the rush of traffic. Delightedly Ellen pointed out the White House, the Capitol, the Washington and Lincoln monuments. She was reading from a guidebook, but it was an old one that hadn't yet included Memorial Park. Near the Lincoln Memorial a great crowd had gathered. Tim parked the car and he and his family got out.

"Is there a concert, Daddy?" Ellen asked.

"I don't know," Tim said.

They listened, but they heard no music. Closer they went toward the Lincoln Memorial. Many, many people were standing, silently gazing ahead as Tim Murphy moved through the crowd, and suddenly he saw it—a long slim chevron of black granite in the ground. He began at one end and followed it deep into the ground, then up and out again, and he gazed upward toward the seated Abraham Lincoln, then to the right the obelisk of the Washington Monument. He was deeply moved by the sweep that the black granite made in the earth, with the green grass and the white granite of the other monuments above.

The names of every one of fifty-eight thousand people lost, killed, missing in Viet Nam had been engraved in white letters upon that black granite. At the left, starting from the first day of the conflict, the names ran in chronological order through the escalations and offensives to the last soldier to die. In awe the people looked upon the thousands of names marching from the war's start to its finish. A hush, similar to that of a church, was upon the crowd as they gazed upon the names of those who had made the ultimate sacrifice for their flag, their family, and their homeland.

Slowly Timothy Murphy approached the monument, following the years along to 1971. Names, hundreds, thousands of names. Among the names he searched, and he knew then, profoundly, that for each name there were hundreds, thousands of stories. Each of these men and women had lived, had shared, had touched other lives in a vast human network, serving their homeland. They were of all shapes, sizes, races, and religions, but they ultimately shared one common fate—they had answered their country's summons and they had fought and died in its service. Fond anecdotes, daring escapes, close calls, thousands and thousands of stories were represented here by those names on the black tablets. These were the sons of fathers and mothers like the Badman's, they were husbands of wives like Paula, and fathers of sons and daughters like Ronnie and Ellen.

Reverently people approached the wall to touch the

names, to reach out and to commune once again with him or her who had been lost so far away and so long ago. They wished to commune for one brief moment with the valor and heroism, the love and the memories of him or her who had departed.

With a start, as Tim ran his hand along a row of names, he saw RAFAEL J. WILLIAMS. *Rafer!* And directly next to Rafer, Tim's heart leaped as he looked at the name in the black granite. ERIC W. BADOWSKY—the Badman. Tim's heart swelled with emotion then, and he reached down to touch those names. Rafer and Badman. He knew they were very near here. He knew their spirits had taken up an abode here with many battalions of other brave men and women. Tears welled up in his eyes as he touched the Badman's name, tears of joy. For so long he had been reaching out, wondering where the Badman was, and now he knew. He placed the picture of the red convertible and the red-haired girlfriend who had married a schoolteacher upon the ground at the foot of the slab, then he held out his own gifts, a white rose and his old headband, The Black Halo. "Take these, Badman," he whispered, "take these for me." And he placed them, too, at the bottom of the slab. He felt a great swelling reverence, then, placing the rose and the headband there, an undeniable, eternal communion with those tens of thousands of spirits who hallowed this place.

Tim turned and nodded that he had found Badman's name. Paula and the children advanced so they themselves could touch the name of the man their husband and father had told them so much about. Paula reached down to Tim crouching there, and she took Tim's hand. As Tim reached to hold her hand in a gesture of triumph, he turned and noticed over her shoulder the bearded, smiling face of a veteran in a baseball cap. The veteran was smiling directly at him.

"Welcome home," the veteran said, and he winked and grinned from ear to ear.

Timothy Murphy nodded, and he stood and embraced his wife and his children. Home. At long last, home.

Thrilling Reading from SIGNET

Great Reading from SIGNET

More Bestsellers from SIGNET